Kiki's
Delivery Service

Kiki's
Delivery Service

By Eiko Kadono
Translation by Lynne E. Riggs
Art by Akiko Hayashi

Annick Press Ltd.
Toronto • New York • Vancouver

Copyedited by Pam Robertson
Cover design by Irvin Cheung/iCheung Design
Cover illustration © John Perlock/i2iart.com
Originally published under the title of "Kiki's Delivery Service (Majo no Takkyu-bin)"
by Fukuinkan Shoten Publishers, Inc., Tokyo, Japan, 1985

Cataloging in Publication
Kadono, Eiko
  Kiki's delivery service/ written by Eiko Kadono ; illustrated by Akiko Hayashi ;
translated by Lynne E. Riggs. — North American ed.

Translation of: Majo no takkyubin.
ISBN 1-55037-789-2 (bound).—ISBN 1-55037-788-4 (pbk.)

  I. Hayashi, Akiko, 1945- II. Riggs, Lynne E. III. Title.

PZ7.K125Ki 2003   j895.6'35   C2002-904899-0

The text was typeset in Revival.

Distributed in Canada by   Published in the U.S.A. by   Distributed in the U.S.A. by
Firefly Books Ltd.   Annick Press (U.S.) Ltd.   Firefly Books (U.S.) Inc.
3680 Victoria Park Avenue   P.O. Box 1338
Willowdale, ON   Ellicott Station
M2H 3K1   Buffalo, NY 14205

Printed and bound in Canada

Visit us at: www.annickpress.com

Contents

1. Bells in the Treetops 11
2. A New Witch's Broom 15
3. Kiki in the Big City 23
4. Kiki Opens for Business 45
5. The Broom Thief 63
6. Kiki in the Doldrums 79
7. Kiki Shares a Secret 95
8. Kiki to the Captain's Rescue 111
9. Kiki Rings in the New Year 125
10. Kiki Carries the Sounds of Spring 139
11. Kiki Goes Home 151

About the Author

Eiko Kadono grew up with stories. Her father did his best to fill Eiko's world with stories of all kinds, especially traditional tales that had been told to him as a child. When Eiko learned to read, she escaped the hardships of post-war Japan by exploring books. Among her favorites were mystery stories by Edogawa Ranpo and Japanese translations of *Little Lord Fauntleroy* by Frances Hodgson Burnett, *The Adventures of Tom Sawyer* and *The Adventures of Huckleberry Finn* by Mark Twain, *Treasure Island* by R.L. Stevenson, and books by Tolstoy, including *Childhood* and *Boyhood*.

These stories and more instilled in Eiko a sense of adventure and a longing to see the world. When she grew up, her dreams to explore came true and she traveled to Sao Pãolo, Brazil. Her experiences there led to her first book, *Brazil and My Friend Luizinho*. She is now a fulltime writer of fiction, and has won many awards, including the Obunsha Prize for Children's Literature, the Noma Award for Juvenile Literature, and a place on the 2000 IBBY Honor List.

"I want readers to imagine the world of the story clearly in their minds," says Eiko. "I hope readers can enjoy traveling to the worlds I create." *Kiki's Delivery Service* is a world Japanese readers have loved visiting – Eiko is now writing the fourth book in the series.

Eiko lives in the ancient city of Kamakura, Japan.

About the Illustrator

Akiko Hayashi has always enjoyed drawing pictures. As a child in Tokyo, she would make pictures of the busy world around her, and of worlds she read about in books like *Fairy Tales of the Brothers Grimm*, *A Dog of Flanders* by Louise de la Ramee, and *La Petite Fadette* by George Sand. Some of these books had illustrations of their own, and Akiko would spend many happy hours looking through them.

At the age of eleven, Akiko's father encouraged her to train with Ichiji Iijima, a local artist, at his studio. From him she learned to watch the sky, the rivers, the flowers, the trees, the animals and the insects and let their dance inspire her art. She has been doing so ever since.

Akiko now lives in Karuizawa in Nagano prefecture, where there is more nature to see.

About the Translator

Lynne E. Riggs was born in Pennsylvania, U.S.A. in 1950. She earned her M.A. at the University of Hawaii in 1976 and began working as a translator and editor in Tokyo shortly thereafter. She coheads the small translating firm Center for Intercultural Communication, specializing mainly in translations of nonfiction literature and periodical articles, and has assisted with translations for the Japanese Board on Books for Young People since 1990. Her translation of Eiko Kadono's "Mirror" appeared in the IBBY anthology of children's horror stories published by Lemniscaat Publishers in 1996.

Chapter 1
Bells in the Treetops

Between the deep forest and the gentle, green hills was a town with roofs the color of toasted bread. It had a train station, a town hall, a police station, a fire station, and a school. It could have been a little town anywhere, and yet, when you looked very carefully, you could see something that wasn't ordinary at all.

Silver bells hung from the tops of the tallest trees in the town. Once in a while these bells rang merrily though there was not the slightest wind. When that happened, the townsfolk would glance at each other and laugh, "There she goes again! Little Kiki is flying too low!"

How could a "little" person ring a bell atop a tall tree? This "Kiki," you see, was not quite ordinary. The house where Kiki lived was over on the eastern edge of the town. On the gatepost facing the street was a wooden sign that read, "Sneeze medicine available here." The green gate stood wide open. There was a large garden, and behind it on the left was a one-story house. The garden was planted with neat rows of rare herbs and medicinal plants, and through its foliage drifted the smell of pungent brews. The smell grew stronger near the house. It came from the kitchen, where a great copper pot was simmering on the stove. On the wall of the living room beyond the kitchen, where in most houses you might see paintings or pictures, hung two brooms, one large and one small, with whisks made of bundled twigs.

From the living room came the sound of lively chatter and the clinking of tea cups.

"Kiki, have you decided when you're going?" came a woman's voice. "I think it's about time you told us. You can't just keep putting it off, you know. You've got to act grown up now."

"There you go again . . . I wish you'd stop worrying and just leave it to me, Mother!" answered a girl's voice. "I'm your daughter, and a good witch. I've got it all worked out, so don't worry."

"Now, now, Kokiri," came a man's voice, "you really should leave things up to Kiki. When she decides to go, she'll go. It does no good to nag, you know."

"Oh, I suppose you're right." The mother's voice was still full of worry. "I just can't relax. I feel responsible, you see ... "

Kokiri was a full-blooded, bona fide witch, the descendant of a long line of witches. Her husband, Okino, was a scholar, a specialist in legends and folktales about witches and fairies. Their only child, thirteen-year-old Kiki, had reached the age when she would leave home and start life on her own.

When a non-witch and a witch married and had a daughter, it was usual for the girl to be brought up as a witch. It was the custom for witches to have their daughters decide whether to pursue witchcraft around the time they turned ten. If a girl made up her mind to become a witch, her mother would begin to teach her the arts that had been passed down.

At thirteen, a witch had to leave home and begin a new life on her own. Picking a night when the full moon shone brightly, she would embark on a journey to look for a town or village where no witch already lived.There she would find a home and a way of putting her witchcraft to good use. Of course, this was quite a big adventure for a young girl. But witches' powers had dwindled and their numbers had drastically decreased, so it was necessary in order to prevent the extinction of their traditions. It was also a good way for people to learn that witches still existed and that they could be friendly and helpful.

Kiki had decided to become a witch when she was ten, so her

mother had started to teach her magic. First, there was the growing of medicinal herbs and the making of sneeze medicine. Second, there was how to fly on a broom.

Kiki mastered the techniques of flying very quickly. The problem was, she sometimes got to daydreaming and forgot to concentrate. Anything could distract her, like a pimple on the side of her nose. Or, she would become absorbed in thought about something, like what to wear to a friend's birthday party.

When that happened, the broom would suddenly begin to plunge downward. Once, she was so self-conscious about her new lace underwear that she didn't notice the broom was descending, and crashed into a telephone pole. The broom was broken into pieces and Kiki got bumped and bruised all over.

So Kiki's mother had picked the tallest trees in the town and tied bells to their tips. If Kiki's thoughts strayed from her flying and she got too low, her feet would strike one of these bells, and startle her out of her daydreams. Recently, however, Kiki's flying had become quite expert, so the bells rang much less often.

Making medicine, on the other hand, didn't really suit Kiki. You have to be patient to grow herbs, grind or dice the leaves and roots very finely, and wait while they slowly simmer in a pot. Kiki never did get very good at such things.

"There goes another witches' craft—lost forever!" Kokiri would wail.

Witches had once practiced many different kinds of magic, but over the centuries, one kind of witchcraft after another had been forgotten. It got to the point that even a genuine witch like Kokiri knew only two magical arts. No wonder it grieved her to see that Kiki took such a dislike to making herbal medicines.

Kiki didn't understand what her mother was so upset about.

"It's lots more fun to fly around than to stand in the kitchen stirring an old pot!"

Then Okino would comfort his wife, "Now, now. It can't be

helped. Maybe some of the forgotten magic will be rediscovered one of these days. And, besides, there're always the black cats, aren't there?"

From long ago, witches and black cats had been inseparable, and in a way, these felines were a form of magic.

Kiki had a little black cat of her own, named Jiji, just as her mother, Kokiri, had had old Meimei. When a witch gave birth to a girl, she searched for a black kitten born at just about the same time, and brought up the kitten with her daughter. Growing up close, the girl and the cat would learn to talk to each other. When the young witch left home to start her own life, her cat would accompany her, her best friend and closest confidant. When the girl grew up and found a partner—in other words, got married—the cat, too, would go off and pursue a life on its own.

Chapter 2
A New Witch's Broom

When teatime was over, Kokiri and Okino went out. Kiki and Jiji sat at the edge of the garden, lazing in the sunshine.

"I guess we'd better get going pretty soon . . . ," murmured Kiki, as if talking to herself.

"That's for sure!" Jiji raised his head and examined Kiki. "You wouldn't decide *not* to become a witch after all this, would you?"

"Don't be silly," Kiki retorted, "I made up my mind, didn't I?" She remembered how proud she had been the first time she had flown on a broom.

Until the age of ten, Kiki's upbringing had been quite ordinary. She knew her mother was a witch, and that when she turned ten, she would have to decide whether she wanted to follow in her mother's footsteps. But she didn't really think much about it.

Then, a while after her tenth birthday, Kiki heard one of her friends say, "I'm going to be a hairdresser like my mother," and it got her to thinking. Should she follow her mother's profession or not? Kiki dimly knew that Mother wanted her to carry on the witch traditions, but she did not think it was right to become a witch just because of her mother. She would be what she *wanted* to be. She'd decide for herself.

Then one day, Kokiri had suggested, "Would you like to try to fly?" She brought out a little broom made just for Kiki.

"Me? Fly?" Kiki had looked dubious.

"Well, you're a witch's daughter. There shouldn't be any problem."

It bothered Kiki that her mother seemed to be luring her along, but the idea of flying was certainly something new and novel. So, after Kokiri taught her the rudiments of takeoff and landing, Kiki got astride her small broom and somewhat fearfully imitated her mother. She stamped the ground with both feet and—lo and behold!—rose lightly into the air.

"I'm flying!" Kiki shouted. She had risen just over the rooftop, and the view made her shiver with delight. The air was slightly blue. She wanted to go higher and still higher. And the higher she went the more she could see. The marvelous, mysterious sensations of flight made her body and her spirits soar.

Kiki very quickly fell in love with flying, and that made her decide to become a witch.

Kokiri was delighted. "I knew you could do it! It's in your blood!"

But Kiki insisted to herself that it wasn't just that; she had chosen to be a witch of her own free will.

"Jiji, let's go take a look now, while Mother's out." Kiki stopped daydreaming and jumped to her feet, pointing in the direction of the toolshed in the corner of the garden.

"Why are you keeping it such a secret?" said Jiji, a little annoyed.

"Well, you know how Mother is about my going. She makes such a big fuss. And she always wants to take over everything—and then . . . things get so *complicated!*"

"Well, I know what you mean. But you've got to make sure it gets plenty of sun to dry it out." Jiji was insistent.

"We'll only just take a quick look."

"Oh, yeah? Are you sure you're not going to take it to bed like before? It'll mildew again."

"Now don't be mean! I can't manage without you, Jiji. And from now on, it's just you and me."

Kiki slipped through the waist-high rows of herbs toward the toolshed. She peered into the narrow space between the toolshed and the garden wall, and let out a squeal.

"Look, Jiji!"

Under the eaves of the toolshed hung a long, slender broom. Drenched in the rays of the evening sun, it was shining brightly.

"It's turned out beautifully. Don't you think it's ready?" Kiki's voice was hoarse with excitement.

"Looks like it turned out fine this time." Peering up from Kiki's feet, Jiji, too, admired the broom. Kiki had tried before to make a broom for flying, but every time she hadn't been able to wait until it dried long enough in the sunshine.

"Hey, Kiki, why don't we give it a test flight? Weather's fine, too. What do you say?"

"Oh, no!" Kiki shook her head. "I don't want to use it until the day I leave. And that'll be soon. I want to start out with everything spanking new. New clothes, new shoes, and this new broom. Fresh and new as a newborn baby. Mother's so stuffy. She always says: 'You come from a long line of witches. You've got to take pride in old things.' But me, I'm different. I'm going to be a new kind of witch."

"Oh, yeah? So how am I supposed to come out 'new'?" said Jiji, twitching his whiskers skeptically.

"You're fine as you are. I'll comb your fur until you fairly shine. I'll make you look all fresh and crisp!"

"Un-huh!" Jiji humphed. "I wish you wouldn't talk about 'fresh and crisp cat' like some sort of dish served up at table. You're not the only one who's setting off to make a new life."

"You're right! Sorry about that." Kiki smothered a smile and glanced fondly at Jiji.

"I wonder how I'm going to feel when we leave," said Kiki pensively.

"You'll probably start bawling, you know."

"Oh, no! You won't catch me crying!"

"So, tell me, Kiki," said Jiji, looking up at her again. "When do you propose to go, anyway?"

"I think I'm ready to leave anytime. Hey, why don't we just go ahead and say we'll go the night of the next full moon?"

"The next full moon? That soon?"

"Sure, that's five days away. Don't you think it's exciting to do something just as soon as it's decided?"

"Oh, I can see there's going to be a big fuss again . . . " Jiji rolled his eyes.

"I'll tell Father and Mother tonight." Kiki gazed far up into the sky and asked, with a grown-up air: "Jiji, what sort of town shall we look for?"

"Oh dear! I wonder what is going to happen? You make up your mind so suddenly . . . it really makes me worry."

"Goodness! What's gotten into you? I'm not the least worried. We can worry when something happens to worry about. Right now, I just feel excited. Aren't you? It's just like when you're about to open up a present."

Kiki's voice sang out, and she reached out and playfully poked the hanging broom. The broom swung slightly as if agreeing with her.

That night after supper, Kiki stood in front of her mother and father and said solemnly, "You don't have to worry any more; I've decided when I'm going to leave."

"What! You decided!" Kokiri jumped to her feet in surprise. "So . . . when?"

"I've chosen the night of the next full moon."

Kokiri hastily ran her eyes over the calendar on the wall. "Gracious! That's only five days away. That's ridiculous! Now wait a minute, Kiki. You'd better put it off until the following full moon."

Kiki rolled her eyes in exasperation. "Just as I thought! Why do you have to make such a big thing of it, Mother? You get upset when I can't make up my mind, and when I finally do, you scold me for what I've decided."

"You know, she's right, Mother. Now take it easy," Okino defended Kiki.

"That's easy for you to say, but she's got to make certain preparations. It's her mother who'll have trouble getting ready in time!" Flushing, Kokiri looked rushed and confused.

Kiki planted herself in front of Kokiri and gazed up at her mother's face. Hands on her hips, she proclaimed in a very grown-up tone, "You should trust your own daughter more! Believe me, I'm already ready to go. Isn't that right, Jiji?" she said, calling out to her cat.

Jiji switched his tail emphatically in confirmation.

"Goodness!" Kokiri's mouth dropped open in surprise, but then her expression changed, and making an effort to compose herself, she asked, "So. What kind of preparations have you made?"

"My broom. I made a new one. Jiji helped me. Didn't you, Jiji? Wait a minute, I'll bring it in."

Kiki opened the door and rushed out to the toolshed. She was back in a flash.

"Here it is!" Kiki held out the broom.

"Wow! You really did make one, didn't you!" Okino was grinning.

"I soaked willow branches in the stream, and then dried them carefully in the sun. Don't you think it came out well? Mother, don't you think so?" said Kiki eagerly, swishing the broom through the air.

But Kokiri slowly shook her head. "You've done a beautiful job. But," she said, "I'm afraid you can't take that broom."

"Why?" demanded Kiki, "I'm *not* going to ride that little kid's broom I've been using all this time. The only witchcraft I know is riding a broom. So I want to have a brand new one I really like."

But Kokiri shook her head again.

"What broom you use is all the more important precisely because that's all you can do. What are you going to do if you make a mistake flying on a broom you're not used to? It's how you start out that's the most important. Going out on your own is not that easy and simple, dear. You'll have a small amount of money, but it will be barely enough to feed yourself for a year, so you'll have to pinch and save. You'll have to support yourself otherwise by using the witchcraft that you know. During this year, you've got to find your own way in life, just like I've been helping the people of this town with my herbal medicines.

"Now," she went on emphatically, "You take Mother's broom. My broom is broken in and it knows very well how to fly."

"No! I don't want your sooty old black broom! I'll look like a chimney sweep! And the handle is so fat and clunky. It's so old and grungy. Don't you agree, Jiji?"

Kiki looked down at the cat at her feet for support. Almost halfway turned around, Jiji purred in agreement.

"There! Jiji thinks so, too! He says a black cat riding on that old broom would be mistaken for a black rain cloud. Riding on the new willow broom, Jiji will look like a prince riding in a glass carriage."

"Gracious! What a pair!" Kokiri burst out laughing. "Listen, you're still just a child. Remember, a witch's broom is not a toy. Eventually my broom will get worn out, and then you can use whatever broom you like. I'm sure that by that time, you really will have grown up." Kokiri closed her eyes thoughtfully.

Kiki pouted, tapping the handle of her new broom on the floor.

"After I went to all that trouble to make this . . . what am I going to do with it?"

"I'll use it in your place. It won't go to waste."

Kiki gazed at her broom for a while and then looked up at her mother. "All right. If you'll use it, I guess it's all right. But for clothes, you've got to let me wear what I want to wear. There's a good dress in the window of the shop on Main Street. It's bright pink, like cosmos flowers. If I wear that, people'll think there's a flower flying through the air."

"I'm sorry to disappoint you, dear, but you can't do that either." Kokiri was looking firm. "Witches these days don't wear pointed hats or long black capes anymore, but witches' attire has to be the blackest of blacks. This is something you can't change, Kiki."

Kiki was sputtering with anger. "That's so old-fashioned! Really! I'll be a black witch with a black cat—nothing but black!"

"That's the way it has to be. It may seem old-fashioned, but being a witch is an old, old tradition, and you'll have to live with that. Besides, you can look quite smart in a black dress, you know. Now you leave that up to Mother. I'll make you a dress as fast as I can."

Mumbling "there she goes again, talking about 'old traditions'," Kiki steamed and glowered, but Kokiri was unperturbed.

"Now, Kiki, you mustn't get carried away by appearances. It's what's *inside* that counts."

"Mother, I know what you mean. You can count on me as far as the 'inside' goes. Too bad I can't show you."

Resigned but undaunted, Kiki slipped around to stand beside Okino.

"Father, I can take a radio with me, can't I? I want to fly through the air with music playing. And I would really like it to be a red radio."

"Hmm. All right, I'll get you the radio you want!" Okino's eyes sparkled as he agreed to her request. And this time Kokiri kept on smiling. Then suddenly she turned the other way, saying, "All right, Kiki, that's enough for tonight. Now you go up to bed." Gathering up the corners of her apron, she seemed to be wiping her eyes.

Chapter 3
Kiki in the Big City

The moon grew plumper each night, until it was full. It was finally the night Kiki had decided to leave on her journey. As the sun began to slant into the west, Kiki and Jiji were clowning around in front of the mirror. Kiki had on the new black dress her mother had made for her, and was turning this way and that, posing and primping. They got on Mother's broom and posed sideways to see what they would look like.

"All right, you two, that's enough of a fashion show," Kokiri called out to them as she bustled about. "Look! The sun is already going down."

"Mother, I wish you'd hem my dress just a little higher," pleaded Kiki as she stood on her tiptoes, pulling up her skirt.

"But why? It looks perfect on you now."

"It looks so *dowdy* this long!"

"That's not dowdy, it's elegant! And you really ought to be as modest as you can. There are plenty of people who'll be critical enough, just because you're a witch."

"Now," Kokiri went on, patting Kiki comfortingly on the shoulder and placing a small bundle next to her, "here are your provisions. I put in plenty of herbs so they'll keep. This is all you can take with you, so make it last. My grandmother used to tell me how her grandmother was a genius at making provisions for maiden journeys. She had a special spell she cast over the herbs she put in that kept the bread from spoiling or even getting stale for a long time. It's really a shame that magic hasn't come down to me!"

"You'd think that sort of thing could be passed down quite easily," said Okino, emerging from his study. "Why would magic like that vanish? I suppose that's part of the mystery!"

"It *is* strange. Even a witch like me doesn't know why. Some say it's because the nights are no longer really dark and no longer really still. There's always light coming from somewhere, and some kind of sound, even though faint, and that makes it hard to perform really sophisticated witchcraft . . . well, that's just what they say."

"It certainly *is* much brighter at night than it used to be," said Okino. "There's always a light on somewhere."

"Yes, the world has really changed," nodded Kokiri, but Kiki, turning away from the mirror, disagreed. "I don't think it's the world's fault at all," she declared. "Witches just didn't try hard enough. Mother's always saying we have to be 'modest' and 'tolerant.' Me, I don't want to have to worry about what other people are thinking all the time. I want to do what *I* want to do!"

"Well, I guess our Kiki doesn't lack for spirit," chuckled Okino.

"Now, Kiki, you listen to me," interjected Kokiri. "It used to be that there were all kinds of people with strange and mysterious powers, but ordinary people always associated such powers with

evil. They believed that magic and witchcraft would bring bad luck."

"That's certainly true," mused Okino, lapsing into thought.

"Absolutely," continued Kokiri. "It's like . . . you know, they once said that witches made mold grow in fresh milk. Then it turned out that those witches knew a recipe for making a certain kind of cheese. That's what they call blue cheese today. And that's just one example." And then, turning to Kiki with a worried look, she continued.

"Witches have managed to survive in a hostile world because they changed their attitudes and decided to live together with ordinary folk, give-and-take. Sometimes it's important to be quiet and stay in the background. Other times, we can come forward and help out. I do think this has been the best way. And things have gotten better: now we even have people like your father, who study and make an effort to understand witches and fairies."

"I guess that was a compliment. Thank you very much," Okino grinned and made a comic bow.

"Oh, goodness, it's gotten completely dark. The moon'll be up soon. That's enough serious talk. We've got to have dinner early." Clapping her hands, Kokiri jumped up, going back to her preparations.

But Okino's expression took on a scholarly look. "I suppose the night of the full moon is convenient for starting out on a journey because it's so bright, but my data on the weather when witches' maiden journeys take place shows it's divided about fifty-fifty between rainy and clear nights."

"Everything depends on luck, after all," said Kokiri, still bustling. "But tonight is going to be fine. The sky is clear. Now, Kiki, are you sure you have everything you need?"

"I hope you find a nice place," said Okino, gazing fondly at his daughter.

"But Kiki, you mustn't just pick any place that comes along," said Kokiri tensely, her nerves on edge.

"I know, Mother. Now, stop worrying!"

"It's not as if she's going to another planet or something. Just another town. And after one year, remember, she'll be back to visit," Okino said, trying to calm their farewell jitters.

But Kokiri just stood in front of Kiki once more. "I know I'm repeating myself, but I hope you'll be very careful about what town you pick, Kiki. You can't decide on first impressions. You should think twice about big cities, even though they look busy and exciting. In big cities, people are too busy to care much about other people. Another thing: when you first arrive, you mustn't appear nervous. Smile. The first thing you have to do is let people know you're not a threat."

"I understand, Mother. Now, I'm going to be all right. Don't worry." Nodding vigorously, Kiki tried to put her mother's mind at rest. Then she turned to look up at her father.

"You know when I was small and you used to toss me up in the air?" she asked shyly. "Could you do that again?"

"Sure!" Okino's voice came out unnaturally loud. Putting his hands under her arms, he tried to lift her up.

"Whoa! When did you get to be this heavy? Okay, here goes, one more time!"

Steadying himself, Okino put out his hands once more and, staggering a bit, managed to raise Kiki up in the air.

"Whee! You did it! But . . . ha, ha! . . . it tickles!" Kiki said, wriggling and giggling in her father's arms.

Exactly on schedule, the full moon rose and shone down brightly over the grassy knoll to the east of the house.

"Well, I guess I'll be off." Kiki had intended to take her farewell properly and formally, but these were the only words she managed to get out. Slinging her duffel bag over her shoulder, Kiki reached for her broom, which was standing nearby. With her other hand she picked up the red transistor radio Okino had bought for her, and then said to Jiji, who had

been waiting quietly at her feet, "Well, let's say good-bye!"

Jiji stood up straight and looked up at Okino and Kokiri.

"We're counting on you, Jiji, to look after Kiki," said Kokiri. Jiji switched his tail as usual in answer.

"Good-bye, Mother. I'll write soon."

"Yes, you let us know how you're doing."

"If things don't go well, you can always come back," said Okino, from the background.

"It will never happen!" Kiki wouldn't think of it.

"Now, don't you go soft on her now," Kokiri frowned at Okino.

Then, as Okino opened the front door, a chorus of "We've come to say good-bye!" arose from outside. About ten people from the town had gathered and were standing in a cluster at the gate.

Kiki didn't know what to say.

"Did you know about Kiki's going?" Kokiri asked them, her voice full of surprise.

"Yes, we heard our little Kiki is going away for a while."

"This is a very special day for Kiki, isn't it?"

"Now you come back sometime, and give those bells in the treetops a jingle."

"We'll be here, waiting to hear your stories!"

Kiki could hear the voices of her friends in the chorus of farewells.

"Oh! You're so nice! Thank you!" was about all Kiki could manage to say. On the verge of tears, Kiki picked up Jiji to hide her face.

"Good thing for this fine weather," mumbled Okino, hiding his own damp eyes by gazing up at the sky.

After many good-byes, Kiki climbed onto her new broom, hung the radio on the broom handle in front of her by its strap, put Jiji behind her, and rose off the ground. As the broom floated up, she turned to her mother.

"Mother! Take care!" If she had said it standing too close, both she and Kokiri would have burst into tears.

The broom dipped and Kokiri cried out in alarm, "Watch out! Keep your eyes on course, for heaven's sake!"

As Kokiri's anxious call echoed behind her, she could hear the assembled well-wishers burst into laughter.

Kiki was relieved. At moments like these, she thought, she felt better knowing that her mother was acting like her usual self.

"Good-bye!" Kiki shouted loudly one more time, then gripped the broom handle and pointed it sharply upward into the night sky. As she rose swiftly into the air, the fluttering hands of her family and friends gradually faded from sight. The lights of the town began to blink and twinkle below her like stars in an inverted bowl of sky. Shining brightly above, the full moon watched over Kiki's progress.

Gradually the lights of the town grew distant until all she could see below were the hunched ridges of the mountains, rushing below her in the darkness.

"You'd better decide quickly where we're going," said Jiji, poking her from behind.

"Hmm . . ." For the first time, Kiki looked around her.

"South. I want to go south. If we go south, we're sure to come out at the ocean. I really want to see what the ocean's like, just once in my life. Is that all right with you, Jiji?"

"Well, what would you do if I said 'No'?" teased Jiji.

"Oh! Come on! Don't say no!" cried Kiki, shaking the broom to which Jiji clung.

"Then why did you even ask me? But remember: What we're looking for is a *town*. All right? Not the ocean."

"Yes, sir! Correct, sir! Now, here we go! To the south! Er . . . which way is south?

Feeling a little silly, Kiki began to glance around the sky, and then, with a sigh of relief, said, "I've got it. That way. As long as we've got the moon on our left, we can make no mistake."

Then, with a squeal of excitement, Kiki gripped her broom and it shot forward, rapidly picking up speed. The wind grew strong in her

face and streamed through the twigs of the broom-
whisk, making a sound like rushing water.

Lights glimmered here and there in the black
mountains below. Sometimes stretches of field,
glowing gray in the moonlight, would loom into
sight, but the land below was mostly mountains.
 Kiki kept on flying south. To the east, the sky began
to grow light, and she watched as the glowing band of white morning
light gradually broadened, chasing away the departing darkness. And
then, what had been a world of gray and dark green began to come
alive in many colors. The low hills were covered with the soft, pale
green of early spring, the green buds like a layer of mist floating
lightly in the air. The rugged rocks of the mountains began to glisten
as if wet with rain, and Kiki's heart pounded with excitement as she
watched the grayish landscape come alive in the early morning light.
 They came upon a deep valley and a small village came into sight,
with smoke starting to rise, first from one chimney, then another. A
small stream winding along the valley floor glistened like a silver
thread in the morning sunshine, and it grew broader until it became
the wide belt of a river curving this way and that.
 "Let's follow that river," said Kiki, "they say all rivers lead to the
sea." She flipped the switch of the transistor radio and began to
whistle along with the music. The broom sped along, propelled by a
strong tailwind.
 "Mother said the big city isn't a good idea, but I really don't want
to live in a small town," said Kiki suddenly, talking to herself.
 "So just what kind of place do you think you're going to find?"
demanded Jiji, raising his voice to keep it from being drowned out by
the wind and the radio's blare.
 "Well, bigger than Mother's town, anyway. I'd want there to be
some tall buildings, a zoo . . . and a train station. And an amusement
park. What do you think, Jiji?"

"You certainly are greedy. All I care about is a nice sunny rooftop . . . a nice sunny windowsill . . . a nice sunny verandah . . ."

"Jiji, are you cold?" asked Kiki with concern.

"A little," came a shivering voice.

"Well then, come up here in front. You'd better learn to speak up when something's wrong, you know. We've got to take care of each other from now on."

Jiji scrambled up Kiki's back, and she pulled him over her shoulder and into the warmth of her lap.

"Kiki, how about that town?"

They had been flying along quietly for some time, when Jiji suddenly stretched his neck to look down at a town passing directly beneath them. Encircled by beautiful, low, green hills, it was perfectly round, with clusters of orange and green roofs, making it look like a bowl of soup dotted with peas and carrots.

"It's pretty, isn't it?" said Kiki.

"That's the kind of town you should pick," said Jiji in a tone of authority. "It's perfect. The kind of town to really settle down in, you know."

"But . . . it's really a bit too small," said Kiki, and then her eye caught something. "What's that, down there!" She was pointing toward a small black speck far below. As they watched, the speck drew near until they could see that it was a witch, flying on a broom, a black cat perched on her shoulder. The witch's broom, however, was jerking and wobbling along like a bucking bronco.

"Shall we go down and say hello?" said Kiki, and leaned the broom downwards in the direction of the witch.

"Well, hello there!" Her broom bucking and lurching without pause, the witch gazed in surprise as Kiki flew alongside. She seemed to be just a little older than Kiki.

"Goodness, I never thought I'd meet another witch in these

parts. Where are you from? Oh! I bet you're a novice witch, and this is your special day. Am I right?" The other witch looked Kiki over from head to foot.

"Yes, that's right. I just set out last night," said Kiki. "How can you tell?"

"Oh, you can tell in a minute! You're all dressed up. And you look a little scared. I was that way myself, so I know."

"Oh, so I do look scared . . . I was trying to look so cool," said Kiki, giggling. And then she asked, "When did you leave home?"

"Just about a year ago."

"How do you like this town?"

"I've only just gotten used to it."

"So, was it hard?" Kiki began to worry, and knitted her brow.

"Well, I managed all right, I guess." The older witch pursed her lips proudly. Then her round face broadened into a gentle smile that left two deep dimples on her cheeks.

This is the face, Kiki suddenly realized, that her mother had been talking about when she said a witch ought to smile.

"So, what do you do to make a living?" she asked.

"I tell fortunes. With my cat, Pupu, here. I can figure out how other people feel, you see, so I have a pretty good reputation for my fortune-telling. It may just be flattery, but the people in the town are really nice to me."

"That's wonderful! And pretty soon you'll be able to go home for a visit, right?"

"Yes. And I can go home with my head high. So I'm satisfied enough. But let me tell you, there were times when the going got pretty tough."

"I can imagine . . . Looks like your broom's got problems . . ."

"What, this?" the dimpled witch laughed, "it's not the broom. It's me. I'm really not much good at flying, but if you don't fly once in a while, you sort of forget you're a witch—don't you agree? And today, there was a cow at the farm on the other side of the mountain that was acting up, and I was asked to take a look. That's what's got me out so early in the morning. I guess you can't call this fortune-telling, but . . ."

"What? A cow?"

"One of the tricks of getting along as a witch is not to refuse any request, no matter how odd it might seem," said the girl. "Cows are sort of eccentric, you know—rather like human beings. This cow, mind you, said she didn't like the sound of the bell hanging around her neck. She was just being ornery!"

"What a thing for a cow to complain about!" Kiki burst out laughing.

"Maybe she just has a sensitive ear. I changed her bell and sang to her for a while, and soon she was back in good humor. Anyway, the farmer's wife gave me some delicious cheese for helping out. It has a wonderful smell, and toasted over the stove, it melts and makes lovely strings."

"How nice!" said Kiki enviously. "Gee, you've got it all figured out."

"You'll be fine, too," said the witch. "You're cute, like I am, and you look at least as smart as I am. You're a bit bold, and good at flying. So do the best you can. I've got to hurry now."

The older witch waved her hand in farewell and, bucking and lurching, proceeded along her way.

"Goodness, that witch was certainly a show-off," Jiji said in a low voice.

"But she said nice things about me."

"Oh, yeah? And that cat! So stuck up! Didn't even say 'hello,' and acted like an experienced know-it-all!" sniffed Jiji.

"Jiji, did you want to talk to that cat? Then you should have spoken up, for heaven's sake! You should be the one to break the ice, you know."

But Jiji had his pride, too. "I didn't specially . . . " he started out, and then snorted.

"Oh, well. Either way, this town already has a witch. Now I've got to think about what I'm going to do." Kiki pulled the broom around to the right and, picking up speed, headed back onto their previous course.

Kiki flew on without stopping. A number of likely looking towns appeared, and even though Jiji complained every time they passed one that they ought to make up their minds as soon as possible, Kiki insisted that she would not stop until they reached the ocean. She kept telling Jiji, over and over again, "it's just a little further."

After a while they left the hills behind them and were flying over fields, small villages, and towns. Now the river was much bigger. It flowed along in a shimmering ribbon, curving in wide bends through the valley. Reflected on the river, the shadow of Kiki and Jiji flying along on their broom looked like a small fish darting through its ripples.

"Hey! Look! Isn't that the ocean?" shouted Jiji.

Kiki had been so absorbed with the landscape right below, she hadn't been looking ahead. Now, she saw far off in the distance a shining line stretching across the horizon, dividing blue sky from bluer sea.

"Yes! It's the sea. You were quick to find it!"

"You mean that's the ocean!? Gee, it just looks like a big puddle." Jiji sounded disappointed.

"What do you mean? Just look! Isn't it wonderful?" said Kiki excitedly, taking in the breathtaking view from one side of the horizon to the other. And then she noticed the houses and buildings that stretched out from where the river poured into the sea.

"Look! See that town?" shouted Kiki. "And there's a big bridge!"

"And a train!" Jiji leaned forward, eyes wide with wonder.

"Well, let's get going and have a look." The broom picked up speed, and off they went.

It was a much bigger town than Kiki had imagined, with many tall

buildings. Gazing around, Kiki announced, her voice quivering with delight, "Jiji, *this* is the place I'm going to choose!"

"Isn't it too big? Don't you remember what your mother said about a big and bustling city?" Jiji was getting anxious.

"But, just look. Isn't it lovely? And look at that tower." Kiki was pointing to a tall clock tower in the heart of the town.

"Doesn't it remind you of a spindle? What fun it would be to take hold of that tower and use it to spin the whole town around, like a top!" Kiki's eyes were sparkling as she drank in the sight below her. "Look, it makes that long shadow! The whole town is just like a sundial!"

"What an imagination!" muttered Jiji, and then he added, almost hopefully, "But there may already be a witch there, like there was in that town back in the mountains."

"We've got to go down and ask before we'll know," said Kiki, and she aimed the broomstick downward, moving slowly toward the central part of the town. As Kiki's feet hit the cobblestones, the street was full of afternoon shoppers. Everyone stopped in surprise and amazement. Some people were frightened and tried to hide behind others, and in no time a crowd of spectators had formed a circle around the new arrivals. Kiki hastily got off her broom, and put Jiji on her shoulder and a bright smile on her face.

"My name . . . is Kiki, and I'm . . . a witch," she blurted out.

"A witch? Well, for goodness' sake! Pretty unusual sight in this day and age!" said an old woman, adjusting her spectacles to get a better look at Kiki.

"Oh! Does that mean that you don't have a witch in this town?" asked Kiki. And then, curtseying formally, she looked around her and announced, "I'm very glad to hear that. Let me introduce myself. I'm a witch, and my name is Kiki, and this is my cat, Jiji. I hope you don't mind me coming into your town."

"You mean you're going to come and live in this town? You're going to live in Koriko?" said a boy.

"Who decided such a thing? That new mayor, I suppose," came a woman's voice. And then the people in the crowd began to look at each other and chatter among themselves.

"Is there something good about having a witch in town?"

"Don't you think it's strange in this day and age—a witch who flies?"

"They did say way back that there's usually at least one witch in every town. But we've never had one before. Never was any problem."

"Mommy, don't witches use magic? Wow! That's neat!"

"Have a witch in town—it should never be allowed! You know they're frightening!"

"Goodness, you don't suppose she's got an evil plot or something?"

Listening to all the talk, not much of it kind or sympathetic, Kiki felt a tense knot forming in her throat. But *I've got to keep smiling,* she kept reminding herself, and then decided she ought to say something.

"I'd really like to live in this town. It's so pretty and the clock tower is so splendid!"

"Well, we're glad you like our town, but . . . "

"But we don't want any trouble, you know . . . "

"Well, you do as you please."

And when they'd all had their say, they scattered, disappearing into the surrounding streets without seeming to care a bit about Kiki.

Bursting with energy when she first arrived, Kiki suddenly felt like a deflated balloon. When she heard there wasn't a witch in town, she had been convinced that everyone would welcome her like something new and novel. But now, the fatigue of flying all night and since morning without eating anything suddenly descended on her. She felt so tired it seemed as if her body might sink completely into the ground.

The people in the town where Kiki had grown up had been happy to have a witch living in their midst. They used to say, "A witch is like the oil in a watch. Just having her around makes the town tick happily," and so she and her mother had been treated very kindly. Almost every day people had come visiting, bringing some delicious treat or part of a gift they had received. In return, Kokiri would give them sneeze medicine, or teach them the names of medicinal herbs used in olden times, or play cat's cradle with old folks living alone, or help out by flying on her broom to bring people things they had forgotten for some important occasion. They had lived in harmony, give-and-take, with the people of their town.

That was the way it had always been since the time Kiki was born, and so it was quite perplexing to be told "Do as you please" without the least offer of help or advice. It left her feeling quite bewildered.

Escaping from the busy streets, Kiki began to wander aimlessly, feeling depressed.

"Well, it's just like Mother Kokiri said," mourned Jiji in her ear, from his perch on her shoulder. "The big city isn't a good idea."

Nodding slowly, lest the tears brimming in her eyes spill down her cheeks, Kiki stroked Jiji's tail. "Hmm . . . I wonder what I should do."

"Well, I'm sure something'll work out," said Jiji, switching his tail mightily and trying to make Kiki feel better.

Evening was coming on. There would be plenty to eat, since they hadn't yet touched the provisions Kokiri had packed the night before. But what to do about a place to sleep? Even if she had the money to stay in a hotel, Kiki wondered if the people in this town would give lodging to a witch. Kiki just wandered along, feeling low and helpless.

"Hey! Is this what witches have come to?" said Jiji, in an especially loud voice, trying to startle Kiki out of her doldrums. "In the old days, a town that treated a witch like that wouldn't get away with it so easily. They'd have their town pulled up by that clock tower and parked on the top of some mountain!"

But Kiki just shrugged her shoulders weakly.

Kiki had no idea where she was, but after walking for quite a while, she had come to a place where the streets were narrow, and instead of tall buildings, there were rows of small houses nestled together along winding streets. The sun had gone down, and the few shops along the street she was on were beginning to close up for the night. People must have been eating their dinner, for the sounds of clinking china and laughter drifted through the windows.

Then suddenly, from a half-closed bakery right in front of Kiki, came a startled cry: "Good heavens! What a thing for that dear woman to leave behind! Listen, you simply must take it over to her." Kiki, thinking she herself was being addressed, stopped walking. But then came a man's voice.

"What's all the fuss about? It's nothing but the baby's pacifier. It's not as if she forgot her baby! I have a neighborhood meeting to go to now, but in the morning, I'll run it over to her."

"But I tell you, it can't wait! She's such a sweet person, and a regular customer, you know. She comes quite a distance, with her baby, to buy our butter rolls. You say it's nothing but the baby's pacifier, but for that baby it's important—same as that pipe is to you! Poor thing, I bet that child won't ever get to sleep tonight. You do as you please. I'm going to take it back to her."

The woman emerged from beneath the half-lowered shutter, and the man's voice followed her.

"Hey! You come back here! How do you expect to get to the other side of the Big River and back in your condition?!"

Indeed, the woman was quite pregnant, and looking as if the baby could be born at any moment. In her hand she held a rubber pacifier. She turned back and said, "Well, will you take it to her?"

"If it's tomorrow I will."

"Huh!" she shot back into the shop indignantly. "Always thinking only of yourself. And to think, you're going to become a father any day now!" Steadying her large belly with both arms, she started down the street, puffing heavily.

Almost without thinking, Kiki began to run after her. "Excuse me . . . If you like, I'll take it for you."

The baker's wife turned around and then took two or three steps backward. She looked Kiki up and down swiftly, and then said, "Dear me! Such a young girl, all dressed in black and carrying a broom—are you a chimney sweep?"

"Well, no . . . actually . . . I've just arrived in this town. I'm a witch," ended Kiki rather timidly.

The baker's wife took another look at Kiki.

"A witch, well, for goodness' sake! Well, a witch!" she repeated in amazement. "I have heard about witches, but you're the first one I've ever met." She took a deep breath. "Are you sure you're not just acting?"

Kiki fervently shook her head. "Oh, no. It's true. So if you want me to take that pacifier to your customer, I can do it quite easily. I would be happy to be of help."

"A genuine witch? Really? But it's rather far, I'm afraid. Is that all right?"

"Certainly. I don't mind, no matter how far it is. If it's not too far north, not the North Pole, I hope. I'm not dressed warmly and don't have a cloak, you see."

The baker's wife burst out laughing.

"Oh, goodness! What fun you are! All right, would you really take it for me?"

"Of course!" Kiki smiled brightly, nodding, and then suddenly became anxious. "Mrs . . ."

"Now, you call me Osono. 'The baker's wife Osono' is what they call me," she said.

"Thank you. Well, Osono, I'm going to *fly* it over. You don't mind, do you?"

"There you go again! It's not so far you have to go by plane!"

"No, I don't mean that. I mean I'm going to fly on my broom."

"What!" Osono looked incredulous and opened her mouth to speak a couple of times, then finally closed it, murmuring to herself, "What a strange day this has been!" She shook her head vigorously and said, "Well, I guess I don't care if you're a witch or a scarecrow, or whether you fly or swim. I just want to make sure this pacifier gets back to that baby."

"That makes me feel much better," smiled Kiki, looking relieved, and Jiji, from his place on her shoulder, swished his tail in a friendly fashion.

"All right, it's decided. So you'd better go quickly." Searching in her apron pocket, Osono continued, "I'll draw a map, all right? And it's not that I don't trust you, but when you've made the delivery, please have the baby's mother sign here and bring the map back to me. And then I'd like to thank you in some way."

Without thinking, Kiki exclaimed, "Wow! I did it!," forgetting for a moment that she wasn't talking to her old friends back home. Then she took the map and the pacifier, got astride her broom, and with a quick stamp on the ground, rose lightly into the air.

"Oh! My! You're really . . . the real thing?" Osono's amazed voice followed after her.

Kiki managed to deliver the pacifier, and the baby's mother thanked her over and over again. "You're a lifesaver!" she said. The baby had been howling loudly, and when she gave the baby the pacifier, it stopped crying immediately.

As Kiki flew back toward the bakery, she began to feel very good. When the baby's mother had said "You're a lifesaver," the chill that had fallen over Kiki's heart had begun to melt, restoring her spirits. To Jiji, who was clinging to her waist as they flew along, she said, "I'm going to be all right. I think you can take it easy, Jiji."

"Oh, yeah!" Jiji was a little unbelieving. "You know, suddenly, I'm very hungry."

"Me too." Kiki reached one arm behind her and patted Jiji on the back.

"When we finish this errand, let's find a nice big tree to sit under and have dinner from Mother's lunchbox. Let's just have a little, though. We have to make it last. It really helps to have the moon so big and bright, doesn't it!"

Osono, the baker's wife, was standing just where they had left her, gazing off into the sky, her mouth still wide open. When Kiki landed gently nearby, she rushed over and said excitedly, "How wonderfully convenient to be able to fly. You really must teach me how."

"I'm sorry, but I can't," said Kiki regretfully. "People without witch's blood in their veins can't fly."

"Oh, is that so?" Osono was crestfallen, but said, "You never know, I *might* have witch's blood. What do you think?" Loosening her arms from her belly, Osono began to flap them like a bird.

Kiki looked down and tried to suppress a laugh.

"No, I don't think you look like a witch."

"Really? How do you know?"

"I just know."

"Oh, dear, how frustrating. But of course—its impossible. I was never told any stories about witchcraft by my grandmother. Oh well. Now," she said, brightening, "what about the baby? What happened?"

Kiki handed the map, which the baby's mother had signed, to Osono.

"The baby was crying but stopped immediately when he got the pacifier back. It made me feel happy, too."

"That's good!" said Osono, "So now, little witch, let me give you some reward."

"Please call me Kiki. And I really don't need any reward. I'm just happy to have met such nice people. That's enough, really. I should be . . . you see, I've only just arrived in this town."

"How unselfish of you. But here. I'm sorry it's only today's leftovers," said Osono, bringing Kiki five butter rolls from inside the shop.

"Oh, how beautiful! I would love to have them," said Kiki happily. Curtseying politely, she picked up Jiji and turned to leave.

"Wait, little witch . . . oh, you said your name was Kiki, didn't you?" called Osono. "You said you'd just arrived in town. Where are you going to stay tonight?"

Kiki couldn't answer. She turned back, still holding Jiji in her arms, and looked forlornly at the ground.

"Could it be you don't have any place to stay?" pursued Osono.

Again, Kiki didn't answer.

"Gracious sakes! Why didn't you tell me?! We have a room—it's upstairs in the flour storehouse. It's small, but there's a bed, and even a sink."

"Really! Do you mean it?"

Kiki almost crushed Jiji in relief.

"If you don't like it, you can look for something better tomorrow."

"Oh no! I wouldn't think of it. Oh, I'm very grateful. I . . . actually, I didn't know what to do. Are, are you sure it's all right? You know, I'm a witch. And I don't think the people in this town like witches very much," Kiki began to feel misery creep up on her again.

"I told you, you're delightful! And *I* like you. Now you just relax. Actually, I'll bet there's even something special about having a witch stay in your house." Osono put her hand under Kiki's drooping chin and, making her look up, winked at her with a warm smile.

The second floor of the flour storehouse next door to the bakery was covered with flour. After Kiki and Jiji had eaten their supper, they crawled into the bed.

"You know, I'm probably going to wake up a white cat tomorrow," said Jiji, gazing at his fur and sneezing a small sneeze.

"But look, Jiji! There's a nice windowsill where the warm sun will shine, just like you were hoping for."

Kiki was happy and relieved. It had been a long trip, but the first day of her maiden journey was about to end.

"Kiki, are you going to look for another town?" asked Jiji.

"No. I think I'm going to stay here for a while. The people didn't welcome me like I thought they would, but the baker's wife said she likes me. Maybe we can find one or two more people who will like us. Don't you think so?"

"Well, maybe. There ought to be at least two or three," murmured Jiji, and with that he was soon deep asleep.

Chapter 4
Kiki Opens for Business

Kiki the little witch and her black cat Jiji had been in the town of Koriko for three days. Osono, the baker's wife, had said they could stay as long as they wanted, and Kiki had spent the whole time in the attic of the flour storehouse. A little at a time, she ate the provisions Kokiri had packed for her and the butter rolls Osono had given her. But she didn't have much of an appetite. She just sat on the edge of the bed, feeling dazed and confused. Jiji seemed to share Kiki's mood. He kept close to her, making no attempt to venture out.

It was about time to go and buy food, but Kiki didn't feel like going anywhere. The constant noise of the city, with the bustling sound of people hurrying along the streets, came through the window and was thoroughly daunting. Everything in the city seemed faceless and impersonal. When she had delivered the pacifier a few nights before, Kiki had started to think she would be able to manage all right here. But the next day, her confidence had vanished.

Since morning, she had been repeating to herself all kinds of lame excuses, but none of them made sense.

"But I just can't . . . I'm not . . ."

She could try living in this town and pretending that she wasn't a witch. If she couldn't stand it, she could go back home, even though it would be pretty embarrassing. But then, she might end up like the bagworm, which spends its whole life in its cocoon, venturing to stick its head out into the world only a tiny bit. No offense to the bagworm, she thought, but I don't want to be like that. Feeling desolate and lost, she gazed idly at her mother's broom, standing in the corner of the room.

I can't just sit here like this, she thought finally. I've got to find something I can do. After all, I delivered the pacifier. Maybe I could do something like that. I'm pretty good at flying. Like Mother said, people in the city are always busy. And here I am, in the big city. Maybe there are people, busy people, who need help with little things. Maybe I could help them. Turning over the idea in her mind, Kiki's spirits slowly began to rise.

Osono came to find out how she was doing, so Kiki asked for her opinion.

"Delivering things . . . You mean a sort of parcel delivery service?" Osono didn't seem to like the idea right away.

"That's right. Except I could carry anything, even little things you can't really call parcels. You know, people could ask me to carry something for them as easily as they might ask the girl next door to do them a favor."

"I see. Now that sounds like a good idea. Yes, come to think of it, that kind of thing would be a big help, even to a person like me. After the baby's born, it won't be easy to go out whenever I need something."

Osono began to realize what Kiki was planning.

"Yes! I think you've got a great idea! Yes, indeed!" She began to grow excited. "So what will you charge? It won't be easy to figure out, if you're going to carry small things like that."

"Well, all I'd really like is to make some kind of trade."

"What do you mean?" asked Osono.

"Well, it's part of the way we witches get along these days. If we can do something for someone else, all we ask for in return is something they have an extra supply of, or a favor—you know, 'give a little, take a little.'" Kiki didn't realize it, but she was starting to talk exactly like her mother.

"Oh, I see. That may be an old custom, yes, but you can't get along on that sort of thing alone."

"But Jiji and I, we don't need much of anything, you know. I have all the clothes I need, as you can see, and we don't eat much. And I'm going to do without things as much as possible."

"I see. That's how you're going to manage," Osono nodded with a look of admiration. And then her mind was working again.

"But if you're going to start up a delivery service, you'll need an office, won't you?"

"Well, maybe just a little one, with a sign that says 'Delivery Service' or some such thing."

"Say, how about right here? The flour storehouse. We can pile all these things over in one corner to make space."

"Really? Are you sure it's all right?"

"Sure! Well, it's probably too small, but in any business it's a good idea to start out small. That makes the process of making it grow bigger all the more fun." Osono's voice was full of excitement as if she herself was the one setting up shop.

"All right. Now that it's decided, the sooner you open up the better," said Osono, "but you know, just calling yourself a 'delivery service' seems rather dull. You need something a little more catchy. You know the thing these days is speedy service right to your doorstep. You should make the most of yourself, you know, you're a genuine witch after all. How about 'The Witch's Express Delivery'?"

"Are you sure it's a good idea to use the word 'witch'?"

"Now come on. Don't be so shy. A business should have a name that's unique. Look at the name of our bakery—Buy, Bye Bakery. People remember the name right away. That's the secret of good business."

Osono gave Kiki a look of firm confidence and nodded vigorously.

It was the next day that Osono had her baby. Kiki found herself suddenly very busy, helping the baker and taking care of Osono. So getting set up was put off for a while but, about ten days later, she finally opened for business.

The flour-dusty front of the storehouse had been carefully cleaned and a sign was hung on the wall:

> The Witch's Express Delivery
> From your doorstep to their doorstep
> Will carry anything faster than any other service
> Telephone 123-8181

With Osono's help, she'd gotten an easy-to-remember number. Kiki and Jiji went out front, over and over, to gaze at their sign.

"Well, we've taken the plunge," Kiki would say, as if talking to herself, every time they had another look. "There's no turning back now."

"That's right," Jiji would confirm, reminding her, "Who was it that was saying how exciting it is starting out something new?"

The "office" itself had all the proper equipment, thanks to the baker. The bags of flour that had been scattered all over the place were piled tidily in one corner, and near the door there was a desk made of a board placed on two stacks of bricks. On the desk was Kiki's brand new telephone and on the wall over it hung a huge map of the town of Koriko. And on the pillar directly opposite the entrance, where anyone

who came in would immediately see it, hung her mother's stout and venerable broom, carefully cleaned and shining. As she sat contemplating the broom, Kiki thought to herself, "It's a good thing I didn't bring that skinny, new one I made. I have enough to think about without having to worry about my broom."

While they fidgeted and hoped, despaired and sighed, a whole week passed without a single customer.

When Kiki went to see the baby, Osono said apologetically, "Maybe it was a mistake to use the word 'witch' after all. Dear me, it's all my fault. I hear people are saying their parcels and packages might have magic spells cast on them and disappear into thin air! What foolishness! If they'd just give it a try, they'd be hooked. If I could only get around better, I'd find a way to help you out," she mourned.

Kiki made herself smile cheerfully. "It's going to be all right. They'll start coming any day now."

But, after she went back to the office, she slumped into a chair, feeling discouraged, and even forgot to eat lunch.

"It makes me so sad. Why do people have to assume that witches only bring trouble?"

"They just don't know any better. There's nothing you can do about it," said Jiji, acting like the wise grown-up.

"That's right. They just don't know. Witches never did do bad things . . . Well, maybe they did things that were unconventional or different. When people see things they don't understand they simply decide they must be bad. I thought that sort of thing had ended a long time ago."

"So you really ought to show them you're not going to do anything bad. Shouldn't you advertise or something?"

"Advertise? What do you mean by that?"

"Like sending out a letter of some kind."

"What would I say?"

"Tell them you're a sweet, harmless little girl witch, and you can do this and this, and so on."

"Hmm. That sounds like a good idea, you know!" Finally the bounce started to return to Kiki's voice.

"So, now to write a letter . . ."

Kiki stood up and opened the window, and a gust of wind blew in suddenly as if it had been waiting right outside to be let in. It wasn't a strong or chill wind, but a gentle spring breeze. As she leaned out the window, Kiki felt the hard, tense feeling that had gripped her heart for so many days finally fall away. Blinking like a mole sticking his head out of the earth, she carefully surveyed the neighborhood.

The windows of all the houses on the other side of the street were wide open. The curtains were pulled back, letting the sunshine flood into their rooms. Kiki could hear the sound of music from a radio carried by the wind, and voices calling out to one another.

Then Kiki realized that a young woman in the window of an apartment house a little ways down the street was waving her hand, apparently trying to catch Kiki's attention. She seemed to be impatiently beckoning Kiki to come her way. Kiki pointed her finger at herself as if to ask, "Do you mean me?" And the woman gestured, "Yes" and, nodding vigorously, beckoned again. Kiki looked at the building quickly, and calculated that the woman was on the third floor, in the fourth apartment from the left.

Kiki picked up her broom and, opening the door, called to Jiji, "I'm going out for a minute. It looks like there's a woman calling me. Jiji, would you like to come along?"

In answer, Jiji leapt up on Kiki's shoulder.

Kiki found the apartment house and went up the stairs. On the third floor she found the door of the young woman's apartment standing open. Inside, the woman stood in front of the mirror, putting on a red hat, a sky blue suitcase in her hand. Seeing Kiki's figure in the mirror, she put down the suitcase and hastily invited Kiki in.

"Oh! Come in, come in. I heard from the baker's wife that you'll carry packages?"

"Yes, that's right."

"She says you fly . . . through the air?"

"Yes," Kiki suddenly felt embarrassed, and dropped her eyes, dreading what kind of comment the woman would make next.

"And she says you'll do it for just a small reward?"

Kiki nodded silently.

"But aren't you a pretty little thing! When I heard you were a witch, I envisioned a creature with canine teeth and horns on her head!" Contrary to her words, the woman actually seemed disappointed.

Kiki was about to utter an angry protest, but quickly stopped herself, pressing her lips together.

The woman noticed her consternation. "Oh, I'm sorry! But you see, there never was a witch in this town before. I've never seen one before. And, you know, in all the stories they're such scary creatures." Without stopping, she went on. "Now, tell me, just how much is 'a small reward'? For air service, I suppose it's expensive."

"No, I'd be happy with anything." Kiki let her eyes fall again, feeling embarrassed by the need to discuss such business matters.

"Anything? How about a favor in return? I'm a seamstress; I sew people's clothes all the time . . . "

Swinging around, she faced Kiki for the first time, and wrinkling her nose, took in Kiki from head to toe. Then she began to shake her head, clicking her tongue disapprovingly.

"That dress . . . well, it's very nice, but isn't it rather long? The fashion nowadays, you know, is to have your hem at the middle of your knee. Say, how about this? I'll be back in three days and then I'll hem up your skirt for you. How will that do for a trade? There, it's a deal!"

Kiki thought it was rather presumptuous of the young woman to decide on the form of payment without even showing her what she wanted carried or where. So she just stood there, her lips set irritably.

The young woman turned back to the mirror and, when she had

finally fixed her hat at the angle she wanted, she began to chatter again, this time even faster.

"I've been called by a client who lives far away and I suddenly have to leave. This client is a most important sort; once she takes it into her head to have a dress, she has to try it on the same day, and so . . . "

Pointing to a bird cage draped with a lace covering sitting on the table, her story tumbled on. "This is a present for my nephew, who turns five today. I want you to take it to him for me. He told me expressly he wanted two birthday presents: a new bird cage and a stuffed animal. And he made me promise not to forget. He said I had to bring them to his house by 4:00 today, and if I was late, he'd make me stand on my head ninety-four times. Now just imagine if you tried to do such a thing! You wouldn't be able to figure out which was your head and which were your feet! So, for heaven's sake, don't be late! There's only one hour left. It's very important. What? The address? Ten Apricot Lane. You go up the river and you'll see the street, behind a big florist shop on the edge of town. What? Name? Just ask for the little brat. They'll know immediately. All right, I'm counting on you. Okay?" Babbling on, barely stopping to listen to Kiki's queries, the young woman gathered up her luggage, handed the bird cage to Kiki, and left the apartment.

Kiki parted the lace curtains of the bird cage and peered inside.

"Oh, look, Jiji. It's just like you! How cute!" Inside was a stuffed black cat with a big peppermint-green ribbon tied around its neck, sitting primly on a silver cushion. It looked as if the young woman had stitched it herself.

Kiki passed the broom's handle through the bird-cage ring, hung the radio above it, and set Jiji on the whisk of the broom, telling him to keep a careful eye on their cargo. Straddling the handle in front, she hurriedly took off from the shadow of the apartment building.

"Wow! It's been a while since we were up. Feels lovely!" The sun had already begun to move into the western sky, and shone brightly in their faces. Jiji was watching from the rear. When the wind blew open the lace curtains of the bird cage, he glared suspiciously at his likeness within.

"Humph! All dolled up with a ribbon!" he scoffed under his breath. And then, a few minutes later, "Look at that silly cushion!" Kiki thought he sounded envious.

"Jiji, would you like to have a cushion like that?" She turned back to him, smiling. "Cushions like that are for stuffed animals, you know."

Jiji acted as if he hadn't heard her. Slowly he was inching closer to the cage. Then, with a flash of his front paw, he snagged the cage and yanked it closer. The broom swerved dangerously.

"What are you doing!" shouted Kiki from in front. "Sit still!" Jiji's ears went up tensely and he withdrew his paw and put it to his mouth.

"Goodness, Jiji. You don't want to get in the cage, do you? I can't imagine why . . . "

"Well, it's a real pretty cage."

"Jiji, you surprise me! And to think, we're the same age!" said Kiki, smiling wryly.

The broom's flight evened out again but, as if waiting for that moment, Jiji reached out again, this time prying open the cage and lunging forward in an attempt to get inside. The broom lurched wildly. Kiki let out a cry, but it was too late. The stuffed black cat fell over, dropped out of the open door, and tumbled through the sky. Kiki screamed and stretched out her hands, struggling to turn the broom downwards to catch it, but to no avail. The toy drifted in a black spiral down, down through the sky.

Kiki changed course, speeding down after it. The forest rushed up toward them and Kiki pointed her broom straight through the treetops. The tree branches struck at her face and body as they descended, and they found themselves in a small clearing, where

Kiki's feet touched down. She immediately set about searching for the toy cat, using the broom to look under branches and in the underbrush.

But the toy cat was nowhere to be seen. The forest was very deep and the foliage of the trees was extremely dense. If it had caught in some branches in the shadows of the leaves, they would never be able to find it. It was just a little stuffed animal, after all, and who knows where it might have been carried if a gust of wind had come along.

Kiki suddenly wanted to cry. Although they had never met before, that young woman had entrusted Kiki with an important errand. It was the first job for the Witch's Express Delivery, and now it looked like it might be a total fiasco. The 4:00 delivery hour was only minutes away. Kiki glared at Jiji, crouching apologetically nearby.

"You sure cause enough trouble . . ."

Kiki stopped, and then exclaimed, "I've got a good idea! Jiji, *you* get in the cage in place of the toy cat."

Jiji's head jerked up with a start and, shaking his head vigorously, he began backing away.

"You wanted to get inside, didn't you? Well, now's your chance," said Kiki sweetly, and then firmly, "Now, get on in. There's no time to waste." Kiki raised her voice and pointed to the cage, her eyes glinting with resolve. Jiji scuttled quickly into the cage, but he did not forget to sit down on the silver cushion, which had fortunately not fallen out. Kiki closed the door of the cage, and then she said, more gently, "This is just for a little while, mind you. As soon as I find the toy, I'll come and get you."

From inside the cage, Jiji looked up reproachfully at Kiki.

"So that means I have to become a stuffed animal?"

"That's right."

"I can't even make a sound?"

"No. Hey! You can just go to sleep. It'll be as easy as pie."

"Do I have to stop breathing?"

"Well, as much as possible."

"But . . . but, oh, no! Remember, he's a 'brat.' That's what she called him. He told her she'd have to stand on her head ninety-four times! *That* kid!"

"Oh, you'll be all right! And I'll come and get you as soon as I can."

Jiji sighed and, looking very miserable, crouched down in the cage, turning sullenly to face the other way. This time, Kiki hung the cage on the broomstick in front of her, where she could see it, and sped off into the sky.

Following the river upstream, Kiki checked the names of the streets posted at the intersections as they flew along. She quickly found 10 Apricot Lane, on the street behind the florist shop. When she rang the doorbell, there was a clatter of running feet, and the door was flung open with a cry, "She's here!"

There stood a little boy. He had a bandage on one cheek, one on the top of his nose, two on his forehead, and three on his knees.

"I'm sorry. Your aunt couldn't come, but I have come in her place. Here is the gift she promised you. Happy birthday!"

Taking the bird cage from Kiki, the little boy looked inside, and then, grasping it in his arms, began to bounce around happily in circles. Through the slit in the curtains, Kiki could see Jiji grimacing as he endured the jouncing.

"Say!" she said hastily. "You take good care of that little black kitten, okay?"

"Okay. I'll take good care of it. I'll be careful. I'll fold it up neatly and put it in my pocket!" And he stuck out his tongue at Kiki.

From inside the cage came a faint, pitiful sound.

"Then I'll be off. See you again!" She waved at the little boy.

"What, are you going to come back and bring me something else?"

"Very likely." And Kiki started off at a run.

Returning to the place they'd dropped the toy, she realized that the forest was part of the park. She began to search carefully and methodically where the stuffed cat should have fallen, but with no success.

If I don't find it, she thought to herself, poor Jiji will have to stay at that kid's house forever. He'll never be able to come back to me . . . he was my only companion, and now . . . She began to feel as if all was lost.

Dusk began to fall in the forest, and Kiki leaned against a tree, tired from her searching. Then she looked down and grasped the hem of her black skirt. I'll just have to cut off the hem of this dress, she thought, and sew a new stuffed cat to replace Jiji. They say short skirts are in fashion . . . so, I guess I'll give it a try . . .

Then, from somewhere behind her, Kiki heard the faint sound of someone talking.

"Which shall I choose? Smoke black is ugly. What I really want is a black-cat black, the black of a witch's cat. Ah! Where will I ever find . . . witch's black . . . ?"

Looking around in surprise, Kiki could see through the trees that there was a small house. What she had thought was a dense thicket of trees was the untrimmed hedge surrounding a cottage. Through the open window, Kiki could see a girl with long hair tied snugly behind her neck standing with her back to the window, painting a picture.

That girl may have seen the toy kitten, thought Kiki, I'll go and ask her.

Kiki squeezed through a small opening in the hedge, and crossed the garden filled with blossoming flowers.

When she stretched up on her tiptoes to call through the window to the girl, she noticed that the painting was of a cat. And then, looking beyond the easel, she gasped with surprise. The stuffed black cat toy she had lost was sitting there in the room.

The girl turned around at the sound.

"Oh! That . . . over there . . . " stammered Kiki.

"Ah! What . . . yes . . . that . . . " stumbled the girl.

And then the two girls looked at each other and shouted at the same time.

"Oh! What a relief!"

"Oh! That's perfect!"

They both took a breath at the same time, and then,

"I'm so glad I found it!"

"I'm so glad I found you!"

And then their words came out at the same time again.

"What?"

"What?"

They asked each other simultaneously.

"I'm glad I found the stuffed black cat," declared Kiki.

"Well, I'm glad I found you, a little girl with a splendid black dress," said the girl.

But since they both spoke at once, their words overlapped, making it come out sounding like,

"I'm glad the black cat found the stuffed little girl wearing a splendid black dress."

Kiki finally collected her wits and asked the girl again, "Did that black stuffed cat by any chance fall out of the sky?"

The girl gazed at Kiki, looking completely mystified.

"I don't know whether it dropped out of the sky or popped out of the earth, but I found it in the woods a little while ago. I'd been looking for a really good black to do a painting for the exhibition for a long time. You know, the real black of all blacks. Ideally, the black that witches use. This black cat seems about as close as I'll get."

Then the girl stopped talking and began to examine Kiki, standing there in her black dress, holding a stout broom.

"Goodness! Could it be . . . ? Are you by any chance a . . . ?"

"Well, I'm a witch," said Kiki, a little reluctantly.

At that, the girl leapt toward the window and leaned way over the sill, reaching out to grasp Kiki's hand.

"Oh! This is wonderful! Listen, you can have this toy cat. I'll give it to you. But come, come inside quickly. And just sit there in that chair, would you please? You know," she said breathlessly, "I've often thought of moving somewhere else, because this town never had a witch living here. And now . . . isn't this great! The witch has come to visit *me*! Do sit down. Please sit down."

Nearly overwhelmed by the girl artist's energy, Kiki had to resist her eager hospitality.

"I don't mind, but you see, I can't now. If I could just have that stuffed animal, I'll be happy to come back later with a real black cat, a real witch's black cat. And then you can paint a picture of the two of us."

"Really!"

"Absolutely. I promise," said Kiki, loudly and clearly. And, taking the precious toy in her hands, she began to run without looking back.

"It's a promise!" the girl's voice followed after her.

By the time Kiki reached Apricot Lane again, it was completely dark. Creeping quietly around the house, Kiki peered in at each of the lighted windows. Finally she found Jiji. The little boy was fast asleep in bed, Jiji pinned tightly in his arms. Instead of being "neatly folded," Jiji seemed to have been neatly flattened, his head twisted backward under the pressure of the boy's hand, his body squeezed under an armpit. There was a bandage on Jiji's nose to match the boy's.

Kiki crept silently through the window, stood up, and pulled gently on Jiji's tail. Jiji didn't move. Could he have gotten a little too carried away with playing the part of stuffed animal? she wondered. A horrible thought started to enter her mind. Jiji was her precious, irreplaceable friend; she'd only now realized just how dear Jiji was to her.

"Jiji, Jiji!" Kiki whispered softly.

She saw Jiji slowly open one eye.

"Come on! Hurry up!" she said, very quietly.

Jiji extracted himself from the boy's embrace and bounced joyfully into Kiki's arms like a rubber ball. From deep down in his throat came a loud purring that was like both laughing and crying all at once. Kiki placed the stuffed black cat in the crook of the sleeping boy's arm.

As he leapt out of the window alongside Kiki, Jiji cried, "Wow! What a relief to be able to breathe deeply again! And move!"

"I know how you feel, but . . ." Not looking directly at Jiji, Kiki went on apologetically, "I'm sorry, but I need your help once more. Well, this time you don't have to pretend you're stuffed. You can laugh or cry as you please."

"Then, whatever it is, it'll be a breeze," said Jiji, looking ready to agree to anything.

But when they got back to the cottage in the woods, the girl made them sit together to pose for her painting, saying, "Now sit straight. I want the witch's cat to curl his tail this way. And don't make such a face. Yes, like that. And don't breathe! Just stay still. Don't move."

Jiji grew so angry his fur stood on end.

But that made the girl all the happier, "Oh! That's perfect! That's exactly what a witch's cat should be like! Don't move! Don't move!"

Sitting primly there with Jiji, Kiki began to feel very happy. Finally, she realized, she had found one more person who liked her.

That night, Kiki wrote her first letter home to her father and mother:

> I've decided to live in Koriko. It's a big
> city near the ocean. At first, I thought it
> was too big a city, but I think the
> business I wanted to start is just right
> for this town. I call it "The Witch's
> Express Delivery" . . .

She wrote about all the things that had happened, leaving out the part about being sad and depressed, and ended her letter as follows:

> Instead of having the seamstress shorten
> my dress, I've decided to have her make
> a silver cushion for Jiji. Then I'll send
> you a formal picture of Jiji on his
> throne.
> I'm doing fine here, so don't worry, dear
> Mother and Father.
> Take care,
> Yours,
>   Kiki

Chapter 5
The Broom Thief

When Kiki opened the door one morning, a flood of sunshine poured in, stopping her in her tracks. She put up her hand against the blinding glare. The breeze was warm and balmy.

Kiki had first come to Koriko in the spring. The sun had shone down lazily, as if it were floating down the skies. It was sunshine not much different from that of the small town nestled in the hills and woods where she had grown up. But now, with the onset of summer, the sun's rays beat down mercilessly, as if bombarding the earth.

Summer on the seacoast is hot, thought Kiki. The heat almost took your breath away. She undid the top button of her blouse and then stretched on tiptoes, peering far away over the distant hills. Oops! she caught herself, I should know better than to think that if I stand on tiptoes, I can see that far. It's all Mother's fault . . .

Back home, there was a grassy knoll to the east of her house that she could see from the front porch if she stood on her tiptoes. In a letter from home a couple of days ago, her mother had written:

> Yesterday, on my way back from an errand, I flew over to the grassy knoll to the east. I remembered that whenever you went out on an errand, you used to stop there, and often ended up coming back very late. Well, the grass was high, almost up to my knees. I sat there for a

while, gazing up into the sky. And then what do you think I did? I went to sleep! The grass smelled so sweet and felt so soft, and a cool breeze was blowing. I don't know how long I slept, but when I woke up, I suddenly realized what I'd done and hurried back home. Your father took one look at me and burst out laughing. He said I looked just like Kiki, covered with chaff from lying in the grass. It made me laugh too!

Squinting into the blazing sunshine, Kiki saw in her mind's eye scenes from the hilly pastures and the narrow streets of the little town where she had once played, and felt a wave of homesickness. Then, yanking herself back to the present, she told herself, "Well, I'd better get to work."

Taking her precious broom, the tool of her trade, off the wall, she began to polish it with energy. This was a task she had performed faithfully from the first day she began the Witch's Express Delivery.

"Well! You're hard at work! Are you working today, too?" Coming out of the bakery next door with the baby in her arms, Osono called out to Kiki.

"You may be getting all ready for nothing today, you know," she said through the window. "In this heat I doubt you'll have any customers at all. The town is practically empty, except for one industrious young fellow sweeping the street over there."

Kiki looked up and glanced along the street. Osono was right. There was hardly a stir in the sweltering sunlight or even in the shadows among the buildings.

"Today's Sunday and it's the height of summer. Everyone's gone to the seashore."

"To the seashore? What are they doing there?" asked Kiki.

"They've gone to swim, of course! Why don't you shut up shop and go yourself?"

"Go to the shore, when it's this hot?" The whole idea was unfamiliar to Kiki.

"Well, of course! You go exactly *because* it's so hot! Oh, it feels wonderful! Living here, if you don't go to the ocean, you'll find the summers pretty hard to bear."

"But I've never been swimming."

"All the more reason you should go, then. I'll find you a swimming suit to wear. When I was younger I wore a black one. After all, it wouldn't do for a witch to go to the beach in any other color, would it? Now, if you wait a bit, I'll go and find it."

"Would you go with me, Osono?" asked Kiki.

"Not with the baby this little. No way. I'd better stay home this year. Getting there will be a breeze for you. On your broom, you'll be there in no time!"

"Oh, let's go together! I'll watch the baby for you," pleaded Kiki, gently brushing the soft cheek of the baby sleeping peacefully in Osono's ample embrace.

"I think I'd rather stay home. But you, Kiki, you haven't given yourself a break since you came here and you've had a steady stream of work lately. You ought to go and have some fun for a change. Just lying on the beach feels really good, you know. Now, wait a bit. I'll bring the swimsuit. If you put it on here, under your dress, all you have to do is take your dress off when you get there." Osono hurried back into the house.

"The ocean . . . " murmured Kiki, turning the idea over in her mind.

"What do you say, Jiji?" she called to the witch's cat, "Want to come with me to the beach?"

Stretched out in a shady, cool spot, looking like a pool of black tar melting along the step, Jiji sounded lethargic and annoyed.

"How can you ask me to go anywhere? Do you know what it's like to be wearing a fur coat in this heat?"

"What's the matter with you? We'll be flying into the cool wind off the ocean, you know. It ought to be more comfortable than just sitting around melting at home. Besides, we've got to give this broom some fun now and then."

"Just now and then, huh?" said Jiji a bit sarcastically through his drowsiness, but he drew himself up reluctantly and began to swish his long tail against his sides. This was Jiji's customary ritual before going out. Kiki smiled fondly and happily at her cat and began to shut the windows of the shop.

Kiki tried on the swimming suit Osono brought. When she pulled the straps up over her shoulders, the elastic suit clasped her body like a tight rubber band.

"Is this right?" asked Kiki, shrinking with embarrassment in the unaccustomed exposure of the swim suit.

"Yes! It fits you fine. Just think, I used to be as skinny as you are. I really envy you, being thin enough to wear that suit."

"But I'm sticking out all over! I don't like it!" cried Kiki, who had always worn long dresses, and had never gone out with so little on before.

"That's the way you're *supposed* to look. Now, when you get down to the seashore, you'll see that everyone else is dressed like that. You won't feel embarrassed anymore."

Osono pulled her skirt up above her knees, and stuck out her own bare leg to show what it would be like.

"Now, off with you, my dear, and have fun!"

Kiki put her dress on over the swimming suit, picked up her broom, hung the radio on the handle, and went outside with Jiji. She put a sign on the door that said "Closed for the Day."

Kiki and Jiji flew through the bright blue sky. The radio was playing a rollicking melody and Kiki let herself sway from side to side with its rhythm.

"Wow! This feels good!" Kiki steered the broom in broad curves to right and left, gliding skillfully on the wind currents.

"It's really wonderful to be able to fly, isn't it! No wonder Osono wants to learn."

Kiki looked down at the city of Koriko stretching below them. The two sides of the city, spread out like the wings of a butterfly on both sides of the river flowing down the center, seemed to be moving in time with the music.

"Kiki," Jiji tapped her from behind. "Listen. There's some kind of report coming over the radio."

Kiki realized that the music had been interrupted and heard the weather reporter say:

> We repeat a special weather warning: Strong storm winds, popularly known "sea-monster squalls," will buffet the coast of Koriko today. Appearing at the height of summer in this region, the squalls are thus named because they come in suddenly, with strong, gusting winds. We ask all swimmers and visitors at the seashore to exercise the utmost caution.

"Listen! It says the weather is going to turn bad," said Jiji.

"How could that be? Just look how clear and beautiful it is!" Kiki paid no attention to the report or to Jiji's worried tone.

"Look! There's the ocean. And just look how many people there are! The weather report has got to be a mistake. Jiji, you have a habit of thinking the worst just as people are trying to have fun. That's a bad habit, you know."

"Well! It's a 'bad habit' to get carried away with things, too," retorted Jiji, turning away from her and ruffling his fur indignantly.

Kiki pointed the broom's handle downward and started their descent. She landed gently at a distant corner of the beach. Who had ever heard of a witch going to the beach? Certainly Kiki never had. So she decided to make herself as inconspicuous as possible.

Watching sideways, Kiki could see that everyone on the beach was absorbed in having fun. Some were playing on the beach, throwing balls of wet sand at each other, burying themselves up to their necks, or sunbathing, stretched out on towels. Others were chasing the waves at the water's edge, or swimming with large strokes through the waves further out. She had never known there were so many ways of having fun at the seashore.

The sounds of laughter and delight and the sight of happy, joyful faces echoed up and down the beach.

The wind began to pick up and the canvas of the beach parasols flapped noisily. The waves had also grown higher, and the shouts of surfers grew louder and more excited.

"Well, I guess we should go join them," said Kiki. Taking off her dress and shoes, Kiki tried to look small as she began to walk across the sand. But she had never walked barefoot on the sand before. It was not yet noon, but the sand was scorching hot. Instead of walking quietly, she found herself prancing in jerks, trying to keep off the burning sand.

They must have made quite a sight. A girl in a black swimming suit carrying a broom, with a black cat at her heels . . .

Trying desperately to keep within Kiki's shadow, Jiji, too, hopped along, mumbling grumpily the whole way.

"Boy! Do you look funny. Like a sesame seed popping in the frying pan. I wish your mother could see you!"

Finally reaching the place where the beachgoers were gathered, Kiki saw how some people had dug shallow holes in the sand to lie in. She found a spot and lay down on her stomach like the others. The sand was as warm as a hot bath and felt wonderful. Feet of all kinds traipsed by her as she lay there, but all of the people were intent on their own fun, and Kiki was relieved to see that they didn't seem to notice much of what was going on around them. Best of all, they didn't seem to notice her.

Kiki put her chin in her hands and gazed at the ocean. The waves swelled up and fell back along the beach, roiling and insistent, like a living creature. The swimmers leaping into the water looked like they were climbing onto the creature's back.

"Do you think I can go in, too?" Kiki realized that her mother had never taught her anything about the ocean. Well, that was probably to be expected. Kokiri herself had probably never even seen the ocean.

Jiji looked up at Kiki with a worried expression. "Kiki, I wish you wouldn't do it. How do we know? It's possible that witches dissolve when they touch seawater."

"That's ridiculous! And just look how much fun everybody's having. It couldn't be that only witches can't go in the ocean. But I'll just see how it feels to get my feet wet."

Kiki sat up and looked off at the horizon. She noticed a cluster of black clouds that hadn't been there a moment ago. In the sand next to her, the breeze stirred up a small whirlwind.

"Look at that! Do you suppose that weather report was right?"

But seeing the sun shining as brightly as ever, she again turned her attention to the people in the ocean, and watched with envy.

Suddenly a voice nearby seemed to be addressed to her. "Hello there!"

Turning to the side, she saw that the woman lying on her stomach next to her was smiling. The woman slowly sat up and pointed to the broom lying beside Kiki.

"What are you doing with that broom?" she asked. "Did you bring it to play with on the beach? In place of a float or something?"

It was such an incongruous suggestion that Kiki involuntarily burst into a giggle. The woman giggled too, and then she said, "Well, I heard that there was a witch in town, so I suppose you're one of the people trying to copy her. But you look great! Me, I'm so busy taking care of my son, I don't have time to keep up with the fashions. I saw a boy with a broom, too, a little while ago."

Kiki hastily tried to hide the broom.

"See him, over there?" The woman turned to point behind her. Beyond the people playing in the sand stood a boy holding a broom and a bundle. He was watching them.

"Oh! He's probably there to pick up trash," said Kiki.

"Oh, really? Is that so? So are you here to pick up trash, too? Somehow I thought . . . " The woman's voice trailed off as she began craning her neck, searching among the crowd. And then, abruptly, she shouted in a loud, screechy voice, "Jonny! You come back here! You don't go so far. Stay there where I can see you. That's right, that's right. You can splash in the water right there where it's shallow. Look, the waves will come right up to you."

When the woman waved her hand, a little boy sitting on a large, orange, platter-like float looking in their direction kicked his feet up and down.

The woman turned back to Kiki and sighed deeply.

"Children are darlings, but really exhausting. It's not easy being a mother!" And then suddenly her voice rose shrilly again, "Jonny, don't go in deep! That's right, you just sit down right there! Now be a good boy."

The woman again looked at Kiki with a smile.

"It would be nice to be able to relax, at least when I come to the beach. Say, how about that kitty-cat of yours. I wonder if it wouldn't play with my Jonny. That looks like a very smart cat. And then Jonny would be sure to stay close by."

The woman reached out to pet Jiji.

Poking him, Kiki said, "Well, Jiji, why don't you go down there and play with him."

Jiji stood up and stretched with a grumbling purr that resounded in his belly. "How can she call a grown-up cat like me 'kitty-cat'? It's downright insulting." Strolling slowly and switching his tail back and forth, he stalked down to the water's edge.

"Wow! What a smart cat!" The woman watched carefully until Jiji reached the place where her little boy was playing, and then flopped down again on her stomach, humming a tune to herself.

Kiki also lay down again, stretching out on the sand. When she closed her eyes, it seemed as if the jumble of sounds mingling around her could be heard all the more clearly. And the smell of the beach—salty, the sea water with its faint smell of fish and kelp—was really very pleasant.

Then, suddenly, there was a resounding roar, and a violent gust of wind completely different from the breeze that had been blowing struck the beach. It hit them as if it had dropped out of the sky. Screams and shouts arose all over.

Blinking the sand out of her eyes, Kiki saw straw hats and floats blowing around in the air like pinwheels. As she jumped to her feet, she could see the whole beach, a peaceful expanse of pleasure until a moment before, in chaos. Parents clutching children close were scrambling toward the pine woods at the edge of the dunes; people chased after belongings whisked beyond their reach by the wind.

"Jonny!" screamed the woman next to Kiki, over and over, and then, suddenly, she started running frantically toward the water. Watching her go, Kiki saw the little boy and Jiji riding on the orange float, being pulled out to sea on high waves. The boy's mother plunged into the surf, but the float kept drifting further out, caught up in the strong, outgoing tide. The boy was screeching with fear. Kiki rushed down to the water's edge and called out to Jiji.

"Hang on tight now. I'll come out and get you."

Then she said to the woman standing helplessly in the waves, "Now don't worry. I can fly. And I'll go out there and rescue them."

Someone close by said, "That's right. Isn't that the witch delivery girl who can fly on a broom?"

"Well, hurry up! Hurry!"

Then Kiki turned pale. Suddenly, she noticed that the broom she held in her hand was different. It wasn't her mother's broom. It was just a cheap, poorly made likeness.

How could such a thing have happened at a time like this? she screamed silently to herself. Who could have switched the brooms? It must have happened during all the commotion of the squall. Or did it happen while she had her eyes closed, sunbathing on the sand? Kiki's heart began to beat very fast. What am I going to do? she wondered.

But there was no time. Quickly getting astride the impostor broom, she took off and, just as she thought she was on course, the tip of the handle dipped down into the water.

"Oh!" the assembled crowd gasped. Kiki gripped the handle and pointed it upward, but then the tail of the broom sank into the water. The whisk quickly became very wet and heavy and tried to pull her back toward the beach. Kiki strove valiantly to gain control, but the broom seemed to have a mind of its own, swerving, lunging, and jerking crazily. And all the while, the little boy and Jiji were drifting further out to sea.

Kiki strengthened her grip on the broom handle and set her lips. She got dunked in the waves and flipped in circles several times, but finally managed to reach the boy. Lying flat along the broom handle, she reached down, but he was crying and flailing about so wildly that she couldn't get hold of his hand. Finally, she grabbed his swim trunks and pulled him up on the broom. Then she caught Jiji by his tail and pulled him up, too. At that very moment, a huge wave

crashed over the orange float and pulled it far out into the dark blue ocean, whirling in circles at a dizzying speed.

The people on the beach sent up a cheer.

Kiki managed to land on the sand. She handed over the limp little boy to his mother and, hugging the also-limp Jiji to her, hurriedly put her dress on over her wet body. Picking up her radio, she got astride the broom and rose into the air.

People in the crowd tried to stop her. "You must be exhausted, why don't you rest a bit. The wind's too strong!"

But Kiki had something more important to worry about. She *had* to find her precious broom, and she had a pretty good idea where it had gone. It must be that boy she had seen through the crowd earlier. He had had a broom in his hand. He must have wanted to have a witch's broom and switched them when she wasn't looking. It made her seething mad. She would never forgive him. Luckily she had been able to save the boy and Jiji, but thinking what would have happened if she had failed made her tremble with horror. She'd find that rascal and make him apologize a million times.

Kiki scanned the landscape below her carefully, lurching along on the bucking broom. Where would somebody go if he got hold of the witch's broom of his dreams? No doubt he would try to find a high place, like a cliff, thinking he would try to fly.

Kiki flew over the small hills that stretched between the city and the beach.

Then Jiji pointed ahead, "Kiki, over there!"

Just as she had thought, there was a figure dressed in black clothing, standing on the top of a high rise, preparing to "fly."

"Kiki, you've got to stop him!" shouted Jiji.

"Shush! Be quiet!" Kiki stopped the broom in midair.

"But he'll get hurt."

"He wants to fly, so let him try! If he gets hurt, he'll learn his lesson. Besides, it serves him right, stealing somebody else's broom!" said Kiki coldly, keeping a firm hold on the bucking broom.

"He's really going to jump!" screeched Jiji.

The boy on the hilltop took off, but instead of flying, he dropped straight down, hitting bottom and tumbling down like a falling rock.

Kiki flew down after him and landed nearby. The broom thief was rubbing his sore behind and trembling with fright and shock. Kiki remarked in a deliberately stern tone, "So! It didn't work, did it?"

The startled face that looked up at her was, as she had expected, that of the boy about her own age she'd seen earlier.

His glasses were cracked and he was covered with bruises and scratches oozing blood.

Then Kiki burst out laughing. She couldn't help it. He had even got himself up in a dress, apparently imitating the one Kiki was wearing.

"Well, it was a good try . . . witch's costume and all," she commented sarcastically.

The boy winced with pain and hastily pulled off the dress, blushing deeply. He stared at the ground.

"I had a terrible time because of what you did!" Kiki planted the handle of the substitute broom on the ground and stood over him, stamping with exaggerated anger. Actually, she couldn't get really angry. The sight of the boy, just as old as she was, wearing a black dress and trying to fly like a witch, was almost unbearably funny.

"I want you to apologize. At least a million times," she persevered.

The boy remained silent and bowed his head. He backed up a step and bent his head again.

"Why did you steal my broom? Most people would have some kind of excuse at a time like this. You don't look like a born thief."

"I'm no thief . . . I was just doing some . . . research."

The boy began to pout defensively.

"What do you mean 'research'?" Kiki demanded.

"Don't shout! I'll tell you right now. Actually, me and my friends in the city, we have a flying club. It's made up of people trying to figure out ways to fly under our own power. Right now, we're divided into three teams, and we're competing to see who can make the most progress in research. One team is studying shoes for flying, the second is to investigate flying carpets, and the third is to analyze the brooms used by witches."

"So, you're on the 'broom team,' I suppose." Kiki stared curiously at him, and the boy nodded with embarrassment.

"Today, I went to your neighborhood and hung around, and then I heard you and the baker's wife talking about going to the ocean . . . so I rushed down here too."

Kiki was incredulous. " You thought you'd just fly on my broom, did you? Well, you can't do anything of the kind! You'll never be able to fly, no matter what broom you get hold of.

"I can fly," she informed him, "because I'm a witch. The blood flowing in my veins is different from yours. So there!"

"You mean," he gazed at her with his eyes wide, "it's blood that flies?"

"Oh, come on! That's crazy!" Kiki burst out laughing, but then suddenly stopped and murmured seriously.

"Well, I don't really know *why* I can fly." She gazed up at the sky and then laughed lightly again.

"The broom does have something to do with it, I guess. If you were going to do research, I wish you'd just concentrated on the kinds of brooms that make it easier for witches to fly. What do you mean, leaving me with this impossible thing? It's hopeless."

"You mean it won't do? I made it myself. I tried to make it as much like yours as I could . . ."

"It gave me a terrible time! It bucks and lunges. It's given me a sore behind, like riding on a bronco. It was really embarrassing, having to fly like that in front of everyone at the beach. Now give me back my broom . . . give . . . ”

For the first time, she began to look around for her broom, and then screamed as she suddenly found it.

“Oh, no!” There on the ground lay her mother’s broom, the handle broken in two.

“What am I going to do? What will I do?” she wailed and, kneeling down, picked up the two pieces carefully and hugged them to herself.

“I’m sorry,” said the boy, bowing his head.

“It was my mother’s . . . I got it when I left home . . . It was really easy to fly with . . .” mourned Kiki, tears pouring down her cheeks.

“I’m really sorry,” he said again, in a low voice, and his shoulders drooped miserably.

Finally, Kiki gathered herself together and realized that no matter how awful it was, what had happened couldn’t be reversed.

“Well, I guess it can’t be helped,” she said in a hoarse voice, working hard to hold back the flood of tears. “I’ll just have to make myself a new one. I’ve done it before, so I’m pretty sure I can do it again. Of course, it won’t be as good as this old one at the beginning, but I’ll get it broken in eventually.”

“I’ve done a bit of research on what makes things fly smoothly,” said the boy, a bit hesitantly. “There might be something I can do to help.”

“Thanks for the thought, but this is a job that has to be left up to a witch,” she said, feeling pride at least in that fact.

“I see it’s not so easy to fly,” said the boy.

“That’s right.” And finally Kiki looked up and gave the boy a smile. “But it’s a pity, too, not to be able to fly at all.”

Chapter 6
Kiki in the Doldrums

The day after the disaster at the seashore, Kiki went to the woods west of the city to cut a branch of horse chestnut and immediately began to make herself a new broom. This time, it didn't even occur to her to try to make the broom smart and slender. She chose wood that would make a broomstick both flexible, so it could maneuver smoothly through stormy skies, and strong and sturdy. After much thought, she decided to keep the whisk of her mother's old broom and reattach it to the new broomstick.

"I'll have half of Mother's broom, anyway," she comforted herself. In a way, the accident had given her the perfect chance to make a completely new broom, but there was something about her mother's that had made her feel secure and safe, and she couldn't bring herself to just throw it away. At least she could use the good, old, reliable whisk.

"Now it's half mine, half Mother's," she told herself.

Sitting quietly nearby with his eyes closed, Jiji opened them slightly to narrow slits to check the progress of the new broom. Seeing what she had decided, he let out a little sigh of relief.

But the new broom was quite rambunctious. Every flight made Kiki dizzy and exhausted. Maybe it was because there hadn't been enough time to let the broomstick dry out properly. Anyway, it would take time to break it in.

The problem was that the whisk from her mother's old broom tended to be more energetic than the brand new stick, so that the

rear end picked up speed before the front
got going, which would cause Kiki to trip
and stumble before she could get into
the air. Sometimes she ended up
practically standing on her head. But
she didn't give up.

Her misfortune had its good
side, too. Now, with her bucking
broom and tumble-down takeoffs,
the people of the town seemed to
care more about her than when she
had flown the normal, graceful way.

"Goodness! Are you all right?"

"What's happened to you?! Have you caught a cold or
something?"

"Have you lost weight?"

"If you're going to fall down out of the sky, be careful how you
fall!"

"We're all quite relieved, you know. It was kind of scary watching
you fly before, like a black arrow shooting through the sky. We
thought there had to be something bad about you."

It had never occurred to Kiki that such bumbling, undignified
flying would actually endear her to the people of the town. Certainly
her mother hadn't been able to predict such a thing.

One day, about ten days after the broom incident, the Witch's
Express Delivery telephone rang. On the other end of the line was
the girl in the forest cottage who had painted Kiki and Jiji's picture
the day of their first real job.

"Hi! How have you been doing? Are you all right? You know that
painting you posed for? Well, I've finally finished it. It's going to
appear in an art exhibition, in fact, and I have a favor to ask. Could
I get you to carry it over to the gallery? I've heard that you do that

kind of job. As you'll remember, it's kind of big, so I hope you'll figure out a way."

Kiki was about to say, "Oh! I'd be glad to!" but stopped herself. Maybe it wouldn't be so easy. She'd never tried to carry a large, flat, heavy object like a painting, and it didn't sound easy. And what if there was a wind? The broom, too, was still not very reliable.

Kiki remembered how one time, after she'd learned to fly, she'd gone to take an umbrella to her father, who'd been caught out in a sudden rain shower. In the middle of her flight, the wind had blown the umbrella open and then started spinning the umbrella and Kiki on her broom around in circles like a windmill. She'd never forget how frightened she had been.

Assuming that Kiki would accept the task, the girl went on. "Since it's a painting of you, after all, you should be the one to carry it. I'm counting on you, okay?"

"Well, I guess I can. I'll figure out a way," Kiki couldn't help but answer, but she was worried.

"Great! So you will come and get it tomorrow around noon? I'll be waiting for you. I'll show you the painting then." The girl sounded very happy and excited.

The next morning, the sky was clear and blue, without a cloud in sight. But that worried Kiki all the more. When you could see so far up in the sky in the morning, there was sure to be a strong wind blowing up there. And towards noon, those wind currents often shifted downward. She knew that from experience.

She began to wonder if she could manage all right. It would be awful if something happened to a painting that meant so much to the girl. Then, suddenly, she remembered something the boy from the flying club had said, about how he had done a lot of research on ways to fly smoothly.

Kiki went to borrow the telephone book from Osono and looked up the number of the flying club. When she rang the number, she hesitated at first, and then asked, "Is there a boy there, studying flying on witches' brooms . . . rather thin and tall?"

"Well, I don't know. Everybody's pretty thin and tall here."

"Oh dear! I don't know his name. Oh, I know. I'm looking for the one with a scrape on his forehead. If the scratches are still there . . . "

"Oh! I know who you mean!" laughed the person on the other end of the line. "Oh, yes, the scratches are still there, all right! His nickname is Tombo. It's Japanese for 'dragonfly.' You know, his glasses make him look like a dragonfly. Oh, there he is. Just a moment please."

"Hello. Tombo speaking," came a new voice over the line.

"I'm . . . This is the witch you met the other day. My name is Kiki."

"Oh, yes! How did you find me? Say, I'm really sorry about the other day. I haven't caused you any more trouble, have I?"

"No. That's all over. But today, I have a problem I need your help with," and Kiki explained about having to carry the painting and asked Tombo what she should do.

"Okay, in that case," said Tombo, grasping the situation immediately, "I think you should use the leash method."

"What do you mean?"

"Why don't you leave it up to me. I think I can help you."

"Oh, thank you! The artist's house is on the edge of the North Park woods, sort of buried in the trees. Do you know it? I'm going over there now."

"Yes, I know the place. Buried like a badger's burrow, right?"

"Yes! Yes, that's the one. So, please come . . . I'll see you there," Kiki began to giggle as she put down the receiver. Yes, "badger's burrow" was quite apt.

As Jiji and Kiki alighted at the edge of the park, they could see Tombo running toward them, carrying a large paper bag.

The girl met them at the door of her cottage. Beaming with pride, she brought out the painting from the room in back.

Kiki let out a little cry of surprise. Jiji simultaneously began to purr loudly. The witch in a black dress and the cat in the painting seemed to be floating in a pitch-black sky. The black was such a shimmering, beautiful color that Kiki, without thinking, had to check the color of her own dress.

"The eyes are wrong." Tombo, who had been silent until then, was looking critically at the painting.

"What do you mean, 'wrong'?" said the girl artist with a start, noticing the boy for the first time.

"Well . . . Kiki's eyes are rounder and prettier than that."

"Oh, maybe I made a mistake. But I wanted to bring out the feeling of the witch in her . . . " The artist made a face and peered curiously at him.

Kiki realized she hadn't introduced Tombo. "Oh! This is a friend of mine, Tombo. He's going to think of a way to make it easier to carry the painting."

Tombo didn't say anything more. Pressing his lips together in thought, he examined the painting again and then went to work. From his paper bag, he produced a handful of different colored balloons.

"Balloons? Are you going to send off the painting with a balloon?" The girl began to look doubtful and placed her hand protectively on the painting.

"Oh, no! Not that way. We're going to put it on a leash." Tombo still wasn't smiling. From the bag he produced a small tank of helium gas and began to inflate the balloons. He tied a string to each one and knotted them together. He screwed a ring into the top edge of the picture frame and securely tied the balloons to the ring. Then he looped a rope over the bundle and through the ring screw. The balloons began to rise off the ground, pulling the painting gently into the air. It didn't rise up quickly or sink down again, but floated calmly in midair, like an obedient dog on a leash.

"The trick," said Tombo, looking satisfied with his handiwork, "is to get the amount of gas in the balloons and the number of balloons just right for the weight of the painting."

"Now, Kiki, you can hold onto this rope and pull the painting along with you like a dog on a leash," instructed Tombo. "If the wind starts to blow it away from you, just pull on it firmly, and it will follow you."

"Like a . . . dog?" The girl gave Kiki a worried look.

Kiki was gazing at the balloons in admiration. Tombo had devised a simple, quick solution she had never thought of.

"It looks like it will work. This will make the painting a lot lighter and it can move freely no matter what direction the wind is coming from. It's a great idea!"

Hearing her praise, Tombo broke out in a smile for the first time.

The leash method proved to be a splendid way to carry the large, heavy painting. When Kiki took off from the ground, guiding the balloon-festooned painting with the rope, it rose into the air with her. She proceeded slowly, letting the wind blow the painting around and around as they went. People walking below, looking out from their windows and sunning themselves on their rooftops, got a preview of the painting of Kiki and Jiji, along with the models in the flesh.

"They're exactly alike! You can hardly tell which is more real!" people exclaimed.

"What an admirable job! Look at that beautiful black dress and black cat!" The painting became the talk of the town.

At the gallery, too, visitors were constantly gathered in front of *The World's Most Beautiful Black*. The girl artist was delighted with her success. She painted a picture of Kiki and Jiji in front of their office to express her thanks. But Kiki's reward was actually much greater because she and her business became known throughout the city of Koriko. It was "advertising" far beyond anything Jiji had imagined.

So Kiki's business became very, very busy. She delivered flowers for people's birthdays, things people had forgotten to bring with them and needed in a hurry, pots of soup for elderly grandmothers living alone, a stethoscope for a doctor on call who had left it in his office. People called on Kiki without the least hesitation. But there did turn out to be some people who had the wrong idea. Kiki said she'd carry anything, so there were calls from a schoolboy who wanted her to carry his school bag for him on the way to school and a person who asked her to deliver an insult. But these requests Kiki naturally turned down.

Finally, the hot summer passed and autumn gradually began to change the landscape of the city. Kiki's repaired broom was now flying relatively smoothly and her life had settled into a regular routine.

But Kiki herself felt somehow irritable and grouchy. She didn't know why, but she certainly wasn't her usual, cheerful self.

Kiki told herself that she had been tense and busy ever since she had come to Koriko; maybe she was just feeling tired. But something else was bothering her, although she couldn't quite put her finger on it.

After she had carried the painting on the leash to the art gallery, Tombo had started coming to visit her quite often. Something he had said on one of those visits kept coming back into her head.

"You're not like all the other girls. Maybe it's because you know how to fly. I can really relax when I talk to you. I don't have to worry about you being a *girl*; I can tell you anything."

At the time, she knew that Tombo meant the comment as a compliment but, the more she thought about it, the more it bothered her that he didn't seem to think of her as a girl.

When he saw the painting, Tombo had said she had pretty eyes, but now, she fumed to herself, he says I'm not like the other girls. What makes me so different? she wondered. She couldn't find the answer and it made her cross and restless.

She was still on edge, too. When a slipper disappeared, she complained to Jiji, "I don't mind your playing with them, but you've got to bring them back here when you're done. How many times have you done that?" she said peevishly. "There's not a single pair left!"

Jiji just pretended he hadn't heard her, yawning ostentatiously.

Then the telephone rang. Hopping on one slippered foot, Kiki went across the room to answer it.

"Hello? Is this the witchery?" asked a cheerful voice on the other end of the line.

"Well . . . I suppose . . ." Kiki hesitated at the unfamiliar question, but she was in too bad a mood to protest.

"I hear that you'll do anything. There's something I'd like you to deliver."

"All right," said Kiki, without much enthusiasm.

"But you see, it's biscuits. My elder sister is Daisy. Now, my name is Violet. You know, a name like Violet just doesn't seem right for an old woman like me!" she tittered.

Feeling impatient, Kiki cleared her throat. What was this woman trying to say?

"Now, I want you to come here first. My house is on Willow Lane. Do you know that street? My house is way out at the end. Number 99. Have you got that, ninety-nine, nine nine?"

"Yes, I understand. I'll be right over," Kiki almost snapped into the phone, and, without asking anything more, she hung up. The call had simply ticked her off all the more and, in a burst of energy, she hurled the slipper she'd been scuffing along the floor into the opposite corner of the room.

Kiki found 99 Willow Lane very easily. When she pulled the rope hanging at the side of the door, there was a jangling sound, and then a voice from behind the house, calling, "Come back here, please!"

Kiki went along the alley that followed the side of the house and found a small, wooden gate standing open. In the garden beyond stood a robust woman with her sleeves rolled up, washing clothes.

There was a line of four large basins, one filled with white clothes, another with black clothes, another with blue clothes, and yet another with only red clothes. Soapsuds shone in the sunlight and frothed into the air as if they were somehow alive. The suds in the basin of whites glistened white, in the basin of blacks shone black, in the basin of blues sparkled blue, and in the basin of reds rose up red.

"Are you Violet, ma'am?" called out Kiki as she entered the gate.

The old woman, absorbed in her washing, nodded her head, the slightly graying locks of her short hair rollicking with the rhythm of her scrubbing. Round beads of sweat stood out all over her forehead.

"I'm the Witch's Express Delivery."

Violet quickly wiped her hands on her apron and looked up at Kiki.

"I thought you were in the 'witching' business?"

"Well, in a way . . . but now I just make deliveries."

"Oh, I see. I heard you were a witch, and I thought you did just about anything. But if you were going to handle every sort of thing like that, my own business would dry up! I'm glad to hear that you just do deliveries.

"You know, I offer a rather unusual service, too," she chuckled with pride, "I'm what you would call a 'make-doer.' When people can't manage in the usual way, I find a way to 'make do' for them. Isn't that rather like what you're doing?"

Violet seemed quite amused with the name she'd given her business and kept chuckling to herself.

"But it's a wonderful help you're giving, really," she went on, turning back to her laundry and starting to scrub the clothes again. "My sister, she's such a stubborn one. If I tell her I'm going to bring her something today, it absolutely *has* to be today. She won't let me change anything. Now, just wait a minute. I'm going to finish this wash. Scrub-a-dub, scrub-a-dub." Violet began to sing energetically as she rubbed soap on a white shirt and scrubbed it on the washboard standing in the washbasin.

"Instead of having to be constantly taking things over there, I'd just as soon move in with my sister. But she says she prefers the freedom of living alone. One more time! Scrub-a-dub! Snap, flap, pang!" She kept time, then went on, "Besides, she can't even bake biscuits.

"Scrub-a-dub. Every week, I take her something and we sit down and chitchat. You know, we have only each other left, we two sisters. Here we go!" She interrupted herself again, "Scrub-a-dub, a-dub. Snap, flap, pang. What's this dirt?! Pretty stubborn spot there. One more time, scrub-a-dub." Violet continued, "But today, I have all this work, and really, I just don't have time to go and see her . . ."

Violet looked up at Kiki again, her stout arms moving incessantly. "You know, it's been raining these past few days, and the laundry work has really piled up. I'm sorry to keep you waiting, but my customers have started calling, asking where their clean laundry is, and I've got to get it done as fast as I can. Scrub-a-dub, snap, flap, pang."

"Are you going to wash all that?" asked Kiki with amazement, gazing at the piles.

"Well, of course. What's wrong? Of course!"

"By hand?"

"That's right. I don't have a washing machine, you see. I'm a 'make-doer,' after all, so I make do with what I've got by using my hands!" she explained cheerfully.

And indeed, Violet's hands were working as efficiently as any washing machine as she chattered away. Kiki watched with fascination. Spreading a piece of wash on the washboard, she rubbed the bar of soap over it once, firmly, then scrubbed it vigorously on the board. Then, holding it on two sides with both hands, she snapped it and flapped it out with a sharp panging sound to knock out the wrinkles, and then held it up to see whether it had gotten clean or not.

"A scrub-scrub-scrub and a snap, flap, pang!" Violet hummed, keeping time with the rhythm of her motions. Soapsuds foamed up and bubbles floated off into the air.

Before her very eyes, Madame Make-doer went through the basin of whites, the basin of blacks, the blues, and the reds. Then, stretching a hose to the basins, she began to repeat the process, rinsing and snapping out the clothes with running water.

Kiki became totally absorbed in watching the industrious washerwoman. She completely forgot that she had come here on business.

Finally, all the laundry was done, wrung out in twists that filled the clothes basket in a huge mountain. At the bottom of the pile were the whites, next the blacks, then the blues and the reds. Violet stood up, put her hands on her hips, looked up at the sky, and took a deep breath.

"All right. Now, let's hang them up to dry."

Violet brought over a length of hemp rope and, taking hold of the end, thought for a moment. Then she said to Kiki, who stood nearby holding Jiji and her broom, "Sorry to bother you, but would you mind holding that end of the rope? I'll hang the laundry on it. With all this wash, it'll have to be a very long rope . . ."

Even before Kiki could answer, she was handed the rope and

Violet began to hang up the wash, beginning with a red ribbon from the top of the pile.

"Start with the small things, then bigger, and bigger," said Violet in a rhythmic voice, as she chose a pair of baby's socks, a baby dress, then a little girl's blouse, pinning them all neatly on the line. With each piece she added, Kiki moved a little further away. The line grew heavy and began to sag.

"Watch out, it's going to drag on the ground!" called out Kiki.

"Oh! What shall we do? Can you stand on your tiptoes?" shouted Violet, as she hung up a large red tablecloth.

"Oh, no! Not that! It'll drag on the ground!" Kiki held the rope high over her head and jumped up in the air.

"Hold it higher. Oh! What will we do? How about if you were to get on your broom?" suggested Violet, gesturing upward.

"Oh, yes. That's a good idea." Kiki nodded, got astride her broom, and floated up to the height of the eaves. Violet bent down again toward the basket and began to pull out the blue laundry.

"Start with the small things, then bigger, and bigger," she hung up a lady's handkerchief, a boy's hat, a man's underpants, a girl's swimming suit, a man's shirt, a blue curtain, and a sky blue sheet, all lined up on the line. Then she started on the black items.

When the laundry seemed about to touch the ground again, Kiki rose up higher over the rooftop. Wiping the sweat from her brow, Violet hung up one piece of laundry after another: a man's pair of socks, a boy's trousers, a woman's skirt, and a lady's dress, all evenly lined up. Then came the white things: baby's gloves, bibs, underpants, shirts, and dresses, from little things to big, a woman's slip, a man's long johns, and, lastly, five bed sheets.

"Finally! That's all!" said Violet with relief, as she tied the lower end of the rope to the fence nearby.

"What shall I do with this?" shouted Kiki, waving her end of the rope from far up over the roof.

Glancing upwards, Violet raised her arms in surprise. "Oh, my

goodness! What shall we do? Maybe you can just find some place to tie it to up there."

"There's no place to tie it up here!" Kiki shouted back. How could she say such a thing? wondered Kiki incredulously. Did Violet believe in sky hooks or something? She guessed that if there was going to be a sky hook, it would have to be Kiki herself. If she were to let go of the line, Violet would have to do all that wash all over again. So Kiki resigned herself to the job of anchoring the clothesline in the sky. Gathering her strength, she hauled on the line and secured it around her waist.

"Wow!" exclaimed Jiji, from the end of the broom, watching the long string of laundry swaying below them like a string of banners, "we have a tremendous, long tail!"

"Splendid!" exclaimed Violet from below, clapping her hands and jumping with glee. "Looks like the banners at a track meet! Ready, set, go! Faster, faster, go, go!" she cheered.

In the streets below, people gazed at the sight with startled faces.

Children started to gather, exclaiming, "Look! It's a kite chain!"

Oh, come on! thought Kiki, making a face. But the tense, sullen line of her lips was slowly curving in a smile, the kind of smile she made when she was really enjoying herself.

"Guess there's nothing to do but get these clothes dry as quickly as possible," she said to Jiji.

Kiki began to fly slowly in a circle over the spot where Violet stood. Flying with the wind in her face, Kiki could feel the breeze blowing away the heavy, gloomy feelings that had made her so peevish.

Kiki began to sing the tune she had just learned from Violet, "Scrub-a-dub-dub, snap, flap, pang!" And from the clothesline below her, she could hear the laundry accompanying her with a melody of its own: "Snap, snap, pang! Flap, flap, flang! Snap, snap, pang! Flutter, flutter!"

The warm sun quickly dried the laundry floating in the clear sky of early autumn. The heavy sound of damp flapping turned into the sharper sound of dry snapping.

"Thank you!" Violet's voice floated up from below as she began to draw in the clothesline. One by one, she took down the wash and, as she went, Kiki spiraled gradually downward. First the whites came down, then the blacks, then the blues, then the reds. They all piled up in the clothes basket in colorful layers and, at last, Kiki's feet touched back down on the ground.

"Look how quickly it dried! This is wonderful! You're a lifesaver!"

"So that's how a 'make-do' professional manages! I get it now: To save time, you 'made do' with me, in place of an ordinary clothesline," said Kiki, laughing.

Making a sheepish face, Violet admitted her strategy. "That's right. That's the way a 'make-doer' makes do! If it works, it makes you glad. If it fails, it makes you sad," she rhymed in a singsong voice. Picking up the huge basket of laundry, she carried it into the house.

Following after her, Kiki found the house full of unusual things. The front door was made up of an upper door and a lower door. You could show just your head, or just your feet.

"The door was broken, so I 'made do' with two smaller doors," explained Violet.

Once inside, Kiki could see that the rope that hung by the front door was attached to a bundle of strings from which dangled an odd assortment of walnut shells, nails, and spoons.

"That's my substitute for a doorbell," commented Violet. "Remember what a nice sound it made when you pulled the rope?"

So that's what was jangling, thought Kiki. And there was also a large black boot stuffed full of fluffy-headed miscanthus grass.

"And there you have a 'make-do' for a vase. Not bad, wouldn't you say?" Fine crinkles burst out around Violet's eyes when she grinned.

"Oh, my goodness, I enjoyed that so much I completely forgot. I was going to have you take the biscuits to my sister, wasn't I!?" Violet pursed her lips, abashed and brought two paper bags from the kitchen.

So, at last comes the job I came here to do, thought Kiki.

"My sister lives on Beech Tree Lane in the apartment house with the steepled roof. And here, here's a bag of biscuits for you, too, by way of payment. I call these Stardust Biscuits. I made a mistake in baking and they came out all broken apart. I hope you won't mind if we 'make do' with a pretty name instead!" apologized Violet brightly.

Kiki was very happy to have the biscuits.

When Kiki arrived at the steepled apartment house on Beech Tree Lane with the biscuits, Violet's sister Daisy sputtered crossly, "Good gracious! How extravagant, to have someone else do one's errands instead of coming yourself! I'll have to have a word with that girl!" But when she peered into the bag, Kiki could see that she was really glad to have the biscuits.

That night, Kiki's office echoed with the refrain of Violet's cheerful song:

> That's the way a "make-doer" makes do!
> If it works, it makes you glad.
> If it fails, it makes you sad.

Kiki and Jiji sang it as they gazed at all the stray slippers, but they couldn't think of any way to "make do" for lost slippers.

Chapter 7
Kiki Shares a Secret

"Knock, knock!"

Kiki was on the second floor when there came a knock at the door of the shop. As she hurried down the steps, she could see a girl in a pink sweater standing there. She had a sweet-looking face framed by brown ringlets and wore shining, white knee-high boots. It seemed to Kiki for a moment that she stood in a kind of aura.

"Oh! Hello . . . there . . . May, may . . . I help you?" For some reason, Kiki felt so flustered she tripped over her words. This was the first time she'd had a customer about her own age.

The sight of Kiki, too, seemed to stop the girl in her tracks, and she drew her breath and looked down at the floor.

"I'm . . . I want . . ." she stuttered, like Kiki had.

"You have something you want delivered?" suggested Kiki, beginning to regain her composure.

"I heard that the delivery service would carry anything. Are . . . you the one who does the deliveries?"

She didn't seem to believe that Kiki was the one who ran the Witch's Delivery Service.

"Yes. It's me. I can take care of it."

"Really?" The girl nodded, and then,

flashing her black eyes, her attitude changed dramatically. She began to bat her eyelashes slowly, as if trying to impress Kiki with her grown-up airs.

"What I want you to deliver," she said, pausing for effect, "actually, it's . . . kind of a secret."

"A secret?" Kiki frowned, puzzled.

"Oh! There's nothing bad about it," insisted the girl, glancing down her nose haughtily and then looking sideways at Kiki. She lifted one arm and leaned languidly against the door post. At the collar of her sweater, the light sparkled on a slender silver broach.

"I want you to take a present to my friend, Lamor. It's his birthday today. He turned fourteen. Isn't that something?" she boasted, as if she had invented the boy's birthday herself. Kiki wondered why the girl was making such a mystery of things. She started to feel very irritated and sharp words rose to the tip of her tongue, but the girl kept on talking.

"But I don't want you to tell him it's a present from me."

"Really! But why?" Kiki couldn't help the teasing tone in her voice.

"It just has to be that way. You see, I've known Lamor since I was little. But now he doesn't think of me as anything but just another little girl. Even though I'm thirteen already . . . "

"Is that the reason you're keeping it a secret? Seems strange . . . "

The girl looked up at Kiki and a proud smile flickered over her face. "What? You don't understand? Don't you know what it's like to feel like this?"

Now Kiki began to feel really irritated. "I don't suppose you've got some weird present in mind—with a frog that jumps out when you open it or something. I don't take jobs like that!"

"Ha! Ha! What do you think I am?" said the girl in a low, grown-up voice. Then she smiled grandly again. "I heard you were a witch, but you don't know anything, do you! Just because I'm about the same age as you . . . What makes you think I'd do anything so silly?"

"How should I . . ." Growing very angry, Kiki glared at the girl but her customer was unruffled. She just flipped her curls and then put her hand into her skirt pocket.

"I saved up my allowance and bought a matching set of fountain pens, one for me, one for Lamor. See!" And she held out a gleaming, silver pen. Then she lifted one side of her collar, revealing its pair clipped underneath. What Kiki had thought to be a broach was actually the clip of the fountain pen. "Having matching pens like this means that we're never apart," she said proudly, squaring her shoulders. "It's the fashion now, you know."

Kiki had intended simply to say, "Oh! I see." This girl was a customer and all she had to do was deliver a present. But when she opened her mouth to speak, she heard herself saying, "But how does that make it a pair? This fellow, Lamor, won't even know the pen is a present from you."

"That's right. All that matters is that I know."

Kiki had sounded cruel and unsympathetic but the girl didn't seem to have heard her at all. She just kept gazing off dreamily into space.

"It's a nice gift. Don't you think you should give it to him yourself? It won't be that hard," said Kiki, a bit too insistently.

"But I just can't. I'd be so embarrassed!"

The girl batted her eyelashes slowly and deliberately. To Kiki, it seemed as if she actually liked the embarrassment. They may have been the same age, but to Kiki, the girl seemed far more grown up, and the thought came to her as an unexpected blow, as if she had been shoved in the chest.

But still she remarked offhandedly, "Seems strange to me, to get all tense over such a thing."

"Hey! Don't you know how it feels?" Smiling slightly, the girl looked as if she felt sorry for Kiki.

Kiki didn't want to admit defeat and retorted, "You're really worried about how Lamor will react, I suppose? After all, he might not care at all. Even I can imagine how that would be."

"Oh, I don't have to worry about that. I just don't want to be obvious. I want to keep it all a secret," she said, giggling shyly.

Kiki looked at the girl again. Inside that pretty pink sweater, she realized, were some pretty complicated feelings swirling around. Is this what "ordinary girls" are mostly like, she began to wonder, remembering what Tombo had said to her. Do you suppose that's why I don't seem like a girl? But the girl kept on talking.

"Don't you know? That's what boys are like. When they only know half of something, they can't wait until they find out the other half. So, I'm going to make Lamor look for me."

"Make him figure out who sent the present, you mean?"

"That's right!"

"What will you do if he doesn't try to find you?"

"But he will. You can count on it!" The girl did not seem to doubt herself in the least.

"Okay. All right. All I have to do is deliver that pen, right?" Kiki had decided she would never understand what the girl was really getting at, so talking about it further was a waste of time. Now, she just wanted to get on with her job.

"Yes, please. And I want you to take this, too . . . " The girl plunged her hand into her pocket and drew out a small, golden envelope.

"A letter, right?"

"Yes, well, it's just a poem."

"Oh! A poem," said Kiki, thoughtfully.

"Yes, I wrote it myself. When you give a boy a gift, you've got to write a poem to go with it. Didn't you know that?"

Not wanting the girl to get the upper hand again, Kiki hastily added, "So, what is his address?"

"On Dogwood Street, on the other side of the Big River, on the west side of the zoo, at Number 38. But in the afternoon, he's usually in the park nearby, practicing tennis by himself.

"And what is your name?"

"My name is a secret. I live on Nutmeg Street, the next street over from Dogwood Street.

"If you're that close, wouldn't it be easy to take it yourself?" Kiki found herself saying.

"But . . ."

"Okay, okay. I understand." Kiki hastily backed off.

"And if you should meet me somewhere in town, by the way, you mustn't let on that you know me," said the girl, and then, "Oh, and, what about your payment?"

Kiki wavered for a moment, then said, "Well, if you don't mind, I'd like to know how it all comes out in the end. Could you just let me know?" As she spoke, Kiki thought to herself that it would be interesting if the boy didn't end up searching for the girl.

"You want to know whether Lamor tries to find out who I am, don't you?" guessed the girl. "You're an inquisitive one, aren't you? Well, that's okay by me. I'll be happy to tell you." The girl seemed absolutely sure of herself.

"In that case, I don't need any payment," said Kiki.

"Really? That's all you want?"

"Well . . ." Kiki was about to try to explain, but the girl cut in gleefully.

"I get it! This is what you call 'research' about boys! Right? I'll bet I'm right!"

Acting the part of the elder, more-experienced sister, the girl nodded knowingly. Bested again, Kiki wrinkled her nose, muttering under her breath so the girl wouldn't hear her, "Who needs it!"

After the girl left, Kiki stood in front of the mirror. She ran her brush through her hair, arranged the collar of her dress in a fashionable curve, and began posing like an elegant lady, pretending to act all grown up like the girl in the pink sweater had.

"What might happen," she paused dramatically, "if this Lamor guy starts to think that I am the girl who gave him the present?

What *shall* I do?" She cocked her head with a mock sigh.

Sitting nearby, Jiji rolled over in exaggerated disbelief. It was highly unlikely.

"Girls! They're so simpleminded!" he said dourly, yawning. "You're hopeless."

"Well, does that mean you're not coming with me?" Kiki put the pen and the letter in her pocket and patted it closed. But Jiji stretched and rose to join her.

Kiki and Jiji took off from in front of the shop. The wind, which had lately grown quite chilly, was strong in their faces. Looking down at the town below, they could see that autumn was well on its way. The ginkgo trees that filled the streets of the town shone in golden glory and, now and then, a stray leaf, swept by the wind, would swirl up to where Kiki flew, and paste itself on her bosom.

"Hey, Kiki! Why are you going so slow today?" called Jiji from the rear. "You're going around in circles, you know."

"Oh! Am I?" Kiki had been lost in thought. She shook herself and checked the landscape below. Ever since the girl left, Kiki hadn't been able to get the letter—and the poem it contained—out of her mind.

When Kiki was very little, she had once written a poem that went something like this:

> Sneakers snicker
> Chocolates chuckle
> Little girls giggle

She had never had anything to do with poetry before or after that one verse.

She knew, of course, that the poem in the envelope she was carrying was nothing so childish. She was consumed with curiosity to know what kind of poem it was that a girl was supposed to write to a boy. She thought that, since the girl had been very pretty and acted so grown up, it must be a very impressive poem. The more she thought about it, the more giddy with imagining she became. As well as she knew that it was wrong to read other people's letters, the more she wished the letter would jump out of her pocket, blow up into gigantic size, and spread itself out before her.

"Jiji, I'd like to take a rest," said Kiki, coming back to reality. "Let's go down to that riverbank there for a minute."

"Hey, we only just took off," protested Jiji.

"Well . . . it's such a beautiful fall." Murmuring the totally irrelevant answer, Kiki steered in a very large arc like a hawk banking in the sky, and began to descend. Her feet touched down in the long park that stretched between the river and its steep embankment.

No one was around. The swings in the playground were swaying by themselves in the wind. At the edge of the park, she could see the steely-blue current of the Big River, whitecaps showing here and there as the wind whipped at its surface.

"Jiji, you can go off and play if you want, just for a little while."

Kiki stood her broom against a ginkgo tree shedding its leaves in a golden carpet and sat down at the leaf-strewn foot of the trunk.

"No, I'd rather stay here. It's cold, so I hope you finish enjoying 'the beautiful fall' as quickly as possible."

"Oh, Jiji. Come on!" How could she get him to leave her alone?

"Why don't you go for a walk," she urged again. "Look, your friends, the kitty-teaser grasses, are all over the place there by the riverbank."

"Are you trying to tell me I'm in the way?" asked Jiji, narrowing his eyes.

"Well, actually, yes. You're in the way!" said Kiki, making a funny face and combing her wind-tangled hair back from her forehead with her fingers.

"Ah! You're keeping a secret from me, aren't you?" accused Jiji.

"Yes. Oh, dear! Is it really so wrong?" Kiki sighed. "Well, it's not like I'm going to break it, or lose it, or get it dirty or something, right? I'd just take a peek, right? Just for a glimpse." She seemed to be trying to convince herself. "Oh well! I'll go ahead and read it!"

"Hey, Kiki! What have you been talking to yourself about, anyway?" said Jiji suspiciously.

"Jiji, now you mustn't get angry. I, well, I just *have* to read that girl's poem. I know it's wrong, but I really want to see it. And you could say it's something I have to know about as part of my becoming a grown-up witch," she finished lamely, watching to see how Jiji would react.

"Do you really have to make all those excuses? If you want to read it, just *read* it! You mean the poem by that stuck-up girl in the boots, right?" Jiji encouraged her without a moment's hesitation. "But, listen, I have to learn the same things, so read it out loud so I can hear it, too."

"Oh! Jiji!" laughed Kiki.

So she sat down and took the envelope out of her pocket. On the front of the golden envelope was an embossed picture of a bouquet of flowers.

"I hope it opens easily," Kiki worried.

Holding the envelope at the edges, she bent them back gently and, much to her relief, the glue separated easily, leaving the envelope open. Inside was a piece of paper the same color as the envelope, folded in half. The poem was written in plump, round letters. Kiki began to read in a low voice:

> Happy Birthday! Congratulations!
> I want to tell you myself,
> But, somehow, I feel shy.
> Happy Birthday! Congratulations!
> I want to look into your eyes when I say it,
> But, somehow, I feel shy.
> I want to give you this gift,
> To put it into your hands myself,
> But, somehow, I feel shy.
> I'm full of glad wishes for you,
> But, somehow, I feel shy.

"Well!" snorted Jiji, "what's all this 'feeling shy' business! Sounds like a scaredy-cat cat."

Kiki put the letter on her knees, which were drawn up under her skirt. Jiji poked his nose in again to get another look and said, "Do you really think that girl wrote that poem? Somehow, it doesn't seem to fit that girl. She acted so sure of herself."

Kiki nodded her head in agreement. "Well, better put this away and get it delivered."

Kiki was holding the envelope in one hand, and was about to pick up the letter with the other when a gust of wind caught her skirt. The letter slipped out of her hand and whirled up into the air. It happened so suddenly, Kiki wasn't prepared. She began to run after the letter as it dipped and sailed through the breeze. Every time she reached up to catch it, it flitted out of reach again. Joining the swirl of golden ginkgo leaves in the wind, it seemed to be playing a game with her. Kiki ran with her hand outstretched, faltered as she missed the letter, and kept on running.

"Kiki! Get the broom! The broom!" shouted Jiji.

Kiki ran back to get the broom but, on the way, she tripped over a stubble of grass and fell down.

"Oh! . . . No!" came Jiji's voice. "Oh, no! It fell in the river!"

Just as Kiki finally got to her feet, she saw the golden letter fall into the water and glimpsed it being swept along in the rapid current.

"Oh! Oh! Oh!" her voice trailed after the disappearing letter, but her feet wouldn't get going. By the time Kiki had started to run along the riverbank, the letter had been carried away on the current and was nowhere to be seen.

"Now what am I going to do?" Stunned, Kiki came to a standstill.

"This time, it's not my fault," said Jiji from behind her.

"That's what I get for reading somebody else's mail. I deserve it," sighed Kiki, slumping miserably. "I guess I'll just have to go and apologize to the girl."

"Well, you could deliver the poem verbally . . ." Jiji tried his best to sound cheerful.

"I don't think that would be a good idea. I think I know how that girl feels, and I wouldn't want another person to deliver that message verbally in my place."

"Okay, then why don't you write the poem on one of those ginkgo leaves? I remember the verses pretty well."

"Hmm. That's an idea. He won't know who the letter's from anyway."

"It'll be a cinch."

"Let's see, it started with 'Happy Birthday! Congratulations!' All right . . . All right, we'll do it that way. Jiji, will you help me?" Kiki began to search around for the biggest ginkgo leaf she could find, and then sat down under the tree again. She took the fountain pen that was to be a present to the boy out of her pocket, removed the cap, and began to write.

"First came 'Happy birthday!,'" Kiki wrote that down, "and then it went, 'I want to speak up myself.'"

"That's right, and then 'But, someway I feel shy,'" declared Jiji.

"No! no! Not 'someway'—it's 'anyhow.' And next was . . . 'I want to look you in the eye' . . . and then again, 'But, anyhow, I feel shy.'"

"That can't be what you call such a good poem," remarked Jiji, "always going back to the same words like that."

"You think so? But I thought it sounded pretty good when I first read it . . . Now, the next part was about the gift."

"About the fountain pen," put in Jiji.

Kiki gazed at the pen she was holding in her hand.

"It certainly is a good pen. It's really easy to write with. So, after that comes, 'A gift of matching silver fountain pen.'" Kiki was gazing up at the sky, thinking hard.

Jiji looked at her. "Hey, I don't remember anything about 'silver.'"

"But I've already written it down. And it *is* silver, so that'll do.

Now, next it went, 'To put into your hands myself'—this part I liked, so I remember it really well. And then, 'But, anyhow, I feel shy' again."

"Goodness, do you think it was that again? Was it repeated that many times?"

"No, it was different. Oh, yes, it was, 'But, anyhow, I still play hide and seek.' Oh, yes, that's right. And then I remember quite well, 'I'm full of glad wishes for you, but anyway I play hide and seek.' There! We've got the whole thing. I've got it all written down." Kiki sighed with relief.

Pushing his nose in to get a better look at the verses written on the leaf, Jiji nodded approvingly, "Well done! Well done!"

The verses Kiki and Jiji produced went as follows:

> Happy Birthday! Congratulations!
> I want to speak up myself,
> But, anyhow, I feel shy.
> Happy Birthday! Congratulations!
> I want to look you in the eye when I say it,
> But, anyhow, I feel shy.
> A gift of matching silver fountain pen,
> To put into your hands myself,
> But, anyhow, I play hide and seek.
> I'm full of glad wishes for you,
> But, anyhow, I play hide and seek.

Kiki and Jiji took off on the broom and continued on their way. Crossing the Big River, they circled wide around the high-rise buildings of the city. Where the crowds gathered at the zoo as it came into view, Kiki began a gentle descent.

Kiki could see the playing field halfway up Dogwood Street. On the dried-out lawn, a boy was practicing tennis volleys against a concrete wall.

"There he is," said Kiki, pointing the handle of the broom downward. They landed in a corner of the field, and Kiki walked up to him.

"Excuse me, I believe your name is Lamor. Congratulations on your birthday!" said Kiki.

"What? Are you talking about me? How do you know so much?" Caught by surprise, the boy's black eyes stared in amazement from his suntanned face.

"You've turned 14, right? But the one who really knows you well is a *certain girl*. I'm just a messenger," said Kiki tantalizingly.

"A girl? Who? Who are you talking about?"

"Yes. Who do you suppose it is? She lives in this neighborhood. Here's a present from her."

Kiki drew the pen and the envelope out of her pocket and held them out to him.

"Wow! This is beautiful! It's shiny and bright like a rocket." The boy held the pen up and flipped it around, enjoying the silver gleam, and then he deftly slipped it into his shirt and clipped it to his collar.

"Oh! Exactly alike!" exclaimed Kiki impulsively, pointing to the boy's collar.

"I wonder if her name is written in this letter," said the boy, turning his attention to the envelope. Then, suddenly, Kiki remembered the ginkgo leaf.

"Wait! Well, if it's all right then, I'll be gone now," she said hastily, and, flushing with embarrassment, she began to walk rapidly away.

"Hey! Just who is she, anyway? Hey! Tell me!" The boy's voice followed her. Not turning around, Kiki shook her head and shouted, "I promised not to tell you."

He does seem to want to know who she is, after all, thought Kiki to herself, remembering the shining, expectant face of the girl in the pink sweater.

Three days later, the girl blew into Kiki's office like an autumn leaf driven on the wind. Kiki felt very bad about having lost the letter, so she just stood there, looking down, afraid of what might happen. But the girl's voice sang out.

"Here I am again!" she said, whirling around on one foot, her white books sparkling in the sun. "I wanted to tell you—Lamor did find me! He said, 'That present was from you, right?'"

"Oh! I'm glad!" Kiki's voice sounded more cheerful than she felt.

"But it's odd, you know. Lamor said something strange. He said, 'That ginkgo leaf. Pretty original! What a neat idea.' Maybe when you were flying along, a leaf blowing in the wind got caught in the envelope. Whatever, it doesn't matter. He figured out it was me! Not from the leaf, mind you, but because of the fountain pen. Because it was the same as mine."

The girl pointed to her collar where the pen was clipped and smiled happily.

Now, seeing the girl looking so elated at the outcome of her scheme, Kiki's resistance to the whole idea vanished completely, and she found herself feeling just as delighted as the girl. And then Kiki decided that she would tell her what had really happened.

"You know, I have to tell you the truth . . . " she began.

But at the same time, the girl blurted out, "Really, I have to confess to you . . . "

"Oh!" they both said, looking at each other.

"Oh, you go first!" said the girl.

"I did something very bad," said Kiki, looking at the floor. And then she explained everything, about how she had read the poem, how the wind had blown the letter away, and how she had written the poem down from memory on the fallen leafs and delivered it to Lamor like that.

The girl let out a little cry of disappointment.

"I'm so sorry," Kiki hastened to say, "but I think I wrote down the poem almost exactly as you had it. When you came here first, I saw you were just about the same age as I, but you are so pretty and you seemed to know about everything . . . so I wondered what kind of things a girl like you would write about . . . I couldn't keep myself from . . . oh! I hope you'll forgive me!"

"Well, I thought the same thing about you," said the girl, "I really wasn't all that sure that Lamor would really look for me. If you'd told him my name, he might have just said, 'Oh. Her,' and never paid any attention. But when I came here, you seemed so very grown up, even though we're the same age, that I didn't want to let you get ahead of me, and that made me act like a braggart. I'm sorry. You and I are probably a lot alike, you know. I'll bet we'd make good friends."

As she had done before, the girl batted her lovely eyelashes and smiled. Kiki smiled back and then she said, in a serious tone, " I am called 'the little witch,' but my real name is Kiki. I hope you'll call me that."

The girl giggled and responded, imitating Kiki's tone, "I am just an ordinary girl, and my name is Mimi. I hope you'll call me that."

Chapter 8
Kiki to the Captain's Rescue

The chill of late autumn set in, and cold winds blew, day after day. The leaves of the trees along the streets had long since dried up and blown away. The color of the town through the window of Kiki's office had turned from green to gold and yellow, and was now mostly a dry, pale beige.

When the wind blew, glancing off the corners of the buildings, it seemed to pierce like a knife. It would suddenly stop, the air becoming very still, and then, abruptly, start blowing again. The sudden gusts made the thin-walled flour storehouse where Kiki had her office moan and creak.

Listening to the sound of the wind, Kiki began to think of home. It was colder in the hills, and there, winter came all at once. By now, the first snow might already have fallen. One day, the wind would grow cold and, before you knew it, the northern mountains would be covered with what looked like a white lace handkerchief. The white lace would gradually extend down the hills until snow had completely enveloped the town. Back in the hills, the first sign of winter was not the sound of the wind, but the whiteness of the first-fallen snows.

Kiki remembered a day of the first winter after she had learned to fly. Kokiri had taught her the tricks of flying when the ground was covered with snow. "The whole landscape turns white," she warned Kiki, "and the dazzling light from the snow can be blinding." And then she had taught Kiki how to recognize the buildings of the town from above by their shapes: the bun-shaped lump was the fire lookout tower, the stair-step-shaped roof was the library, and the square shape was the gymnasium.

Sitting in her office, Kiki pulled her sleeves down over her hands, trying to keep them warm.

"Witches are supposed to be tough against the cold," she shivered, "but this chill cuts right through you."

"That's what you get," said Jiji cheekily, "for just sitting here, doing nothing." He himself was snuggled tightly in a ball on Kiki's lap.

Maybe the cold made people want to keep to themselves. Or maybe they just didn't want any extra bother. Kiki's business had slowed to a trickle.

What I'd really like to do now, she was thinking, is wrap myself in a blanket and chitchat with Kokiri over a nice cup of saffron tea. As she remembered the fragrance of thick, yellow tea, Kiki felt how much she missed her mother.

"I wonder when you plant saffron?" Kiki murmured, mostly to herself. She was beginning to regret that she had not gotten her mother to teach her more about the herbs and medicinal plants she planted and harvested each year. How was it that she made the red-pepper poultice? Did she boil the peppers or roast them? What was it she put in the vegetable soup she made whenever I got a stomachache? What was it?

Trying to remember the things she had always watched Kokiri doing, Kiki realized that she couldn't remember a single one very clearly. Why didn't I pay any more attention to what Mother and Father were doing? It seemed very strange, now that she thought about it, that she would ever forget. Grimacing, she closed her eyes for a moment.

Suddenly there was a gust of wind, and when Kiki looked around, she could see that the front door had been opened a crack. Two pairs of eyes stared through the crack and there was the sound of voices.

"Look! They say a witch cat's eyes glow green like flashlights when it gets cold, but that's all wrong. See, they're just like an ordinary cat's."

"What? What? Let me see. Oh! You're right. Then, maybe it breathes fire. You know, the boy next door told me you can start a fire with a witch's cat. Let's get a better look!"

Jiji looked up at Kiki and then gazed at the door, glaring with big, round eyes, and then opened his mouth, showing his teeth, and let out a fearful hiss.

"Eek!" came the voices and the door slammed shut.

"Did you see that?" said a small voice.

"Yeah. But there weren't any sparks," said another voice.

"And its eyes didn't shine like flashlights."

"They didn't even glimmer."

"It's just a black, black cat, after all."

And then the patter of small children's feet faded down the street.

"Isn't that too bad, I'm just a plain black cat!" complained Jiji with exasperation, "I'm getting really tired of those neighbor kids peeking in on us like that." In a moment he was curled up again on Kiki's warm lap.

"It's a rough life being so popular, isn't it, ol' Jiji?" teased Kiki, batting her eyelashes at her cat saucily. "Maybe you should just take advantage of it. You know, go for the really 'far out' look. Dye your fur red. Wear sunglasses. You'd be a real hit."

Jiji gave Kiki one scathing look and then decided to ignore her.

The telephone rang.

"Well, you don't suppose it's work, do you?" said Kiki, picking up the telephone. The voice on the other end of the line spoke very slowly, with pauses between words.

"Is this . . . the Witch's . . . Express? Well, I . . . have . . . a favor . . . to ask. I'm . . . the grandmother . . . of this . . . house. Oh! Just . . . wait . . . a minute . . . please. The receiver . . . under my chin . . . is about to . . . fall. You see . . . I'm very busy . . . knitting . . . Both hands . . . are full . . . I'm . . . Granny . . . on Jellybean Tree Lane . . . at Number 4 . . . Please . . . come . . . "

"All right . . . I understand . . . I'll be right . . . over," Kiki found the old lady's jerky cadence infectious.

Kiki and Jiji flew over to what the old woman had called Number 4 on Jellybean Tree Lane, and found it was a house on the edge of a small branch of the Big River. It was a tiny house, with a tiny sky-blue painted dock on the water's edge. Inside, there was a tiny, old woman perched on a big, wooden chair, knitting at lightning speed.

"Could you . . . please . . . just wait . . . a minute . . . I'm . . . nearly . . . finished knitting . . . this bellyband," the old woman said slowly, matching her words with the timing of her needles.

"I said . . . to my son . . . I was . . . almost . . . finished . . . he should wait . . . but he . . . just left . . . anyway. Said he . . . didn't need . . . it. Said . . . it was . . . silly. That child! He's still . . . rebelling . . . There . . . it's done!"

Cutting the thread with the scissors, the old woman twisted her head and shoulders this way and that, "Goodness! That was exhausting!" And then, catching Kiki's eye, she began to talk at normal speed.

"Now, Miss Express Delivery Girl, how is *your* tummy?"

"Oh, thank you, I just had something to eat, so I'm not hungry." Kiki stood on her tiptoes and energetically stretched tall to show how good she felt.

"No, no! I don't mean that, I'm asking if your stomach doesn't hurt."

"Not at all. I'm feeling very fine. I can go as far as you need me to," said Kiki again, earnestly.

"It's exactly when you're feeling fine that you've really got to be careful," warned Granny, with concern. "You mustn't let your tummy take a chill. The only way to keep healthy is to keep it warm at *all* times. Nothing's more important than taking good care of your tummy. I'm telling you. The belly is the center of the universe, after all. A bellyband is the perfect thing. And a good bellyband is knit with many bright colors and plenty of thick stitches to make it soft and warm. Don't you agree?" Granny concluded with look of great satisfaction, and then she turned to Jiji, who was sitting at Kiki's feet.

"Oh! How about you? How's *your* tummy?"

By way of answer, Jiji rumbled a loud purr from deep in his chest.

"Oh! Gracious! That sound is proof your tummy's got a chill. Now, let me see. Somewhere, there's got to be a bellyband just right for a little black kitty."

Granny began to look about among the things around the house, and then Kiki noticed that everything was cozily snuggled in stretchy, thick-pile, hand-knit bellybands. The telephone, the coffee cups, the coffee pot, the medicine bottles, the tea kettle, the thermos bottle, the tea caddy, the boots in the entryway, the flowerpots, and even the walking cane.

"There! That's just the one."

Getting up from her chair, Granny went over and took the bellyband off the thermos bottle.

"Here," she said, taking it over and slipping it onto Jiji's furry torso. "The thermos bottle can take care of itself, and this bellyband is not only warm, it's knit in my special 'magic' pattern—polka dots on the outside and stripes on the inside—just right for a black witch's cat!" Granny's face crinkled with delight at her choice.

Indeed, the bellyband she had put on Jiji was lovely. It was made with a mixture of pink and lighter pink yarn. The outside was like a field of apricot blossoms and the inside was striped, like the dawn swept by the mists of spring.

"Oh! How pretty!" exclaimed Kiki. And then she told her cat, "It really looks nice on you, Jiji."

But Jiji was not pleased. His tail went straight up and he turned his head away, looking alarmed at the thing that clasped his belly, and tried to edge away, with comically stiff, ginger steps.

"And I'll knit one for you, too, my dear. I know two bellybands isn't much by way of payment for your services, but I'd be grateful if you'd let that do . . ." said Granny, looking apologetic.

"Oh, that will be fine, of course." Kiki smiled happily at the offer, and that made Granny smile, too. Then she began to chatter again.

"As long as you wear a bellyband, you have nothing to worry about," she said firmly. "There's no better or more economical a way of staying healthy. Why, just the other day, I recommended it to the mayor. He's got a naughty side to him, you know, so I told him it was the secret to keeping his mischievous imps under control. After all, he's the mayor, and he's got to project the right image. It's the secret, I told him, to popularity and success.

"Besides, did you know that there was an epidemic of tummy chills among the animals in the zoo last winter? I *told* them that all the animals in the zoo should have bellybands, but that old zookeeper, he's as obstinate as my son, he didn't pay any attention to me . . . This year, no matter what anybody says, I'm going to make all those animals bellybands and take them over there myself."

Beads of sweat broke out on Granny's small, determined face.

"Ah! Now I know what you want me to deliver!" exclaimed Kiki. "That bellyband you just finished, it's for the elephant at the zoo, I'll bet," she said, pointing to the voluminous folds Granny had just completed. The pattern was a mixture of sky-blue and white stripes, like clouds scattered across a bright, blue sky. Kiki had been wondering from the time she came in why Granny was knitting such a huge belly warmer.

"No. This is for my son. He's the captain of a tum-tum steamboat. He said he had very, very *precious* cargo today. It had to be taken over to Morimo Point at the mouth of Koriko Bay, and he left at the crack of dawn. And what do you think was so *precious*? It was a load of some kind of high-class wine in big, bulbous bottles. He says they have to be carried gently, or the wine's taste could easily go bad. I never heard of such a thing."

Granny pursed her lips in perplexity, and went on. "To get to Morimo Point, you know, you have to drive over two hills, so I guess they figured there'd be less bumping if the wine went by sea. But the waves on the ocean can be a lot bumpier than two hills, if you ask me. Do you suppose they'll be all right?"

Granny drew her breath and, without waiting for Kiki to reply, continued her story.

"So that's why I called you. My son's boat is a tum-tum steamboat called the *Te-te*, and that boat is getting on in age, just like me. She's quite a granny. And these days, she can't seem to keep up her tum-tum tune. It's more like a sort of "tum-ah-tum, tum-ah-tum"—the sure sign of fatigue. There's still smoke coming out of the chimney, of course, but I tell you, that engine's under the weather . . . So anyway, what I want you to do is take this belly warmer over to the ship, because the *Te-te* has a very important job to do. I've already told my son he ought to use it . . . If you just follow along the edge of the Big River, I think you'll find the ship soon enough. It's such a bother, I know, and I'm sorry to put you out, but that boy, he just won't listen to me!" Granny sighed and shrugged her shoulders.

Holding the bulky knitting in her arms, Kiki could not help wondering to herself: How could this tiny woman have a son that would need such a billowing bellyband as this? But she did not have time to ask. Granny started talking again, "Now, if my son makes a fuss, I want you to just put it on anyway. If it's too big, you can take a tuck here and there, and if it's too small, just stretch it out. It'll fit fine."

Kiki was still feeling dubious, but she smiled brightly to reassure Granny. "All right, I understand."

Draping the bellyband around her shoulders like a cape, Kiki took flight. "Oh! That was a good idea. This is nice and warm," she remarked to herself.

Behind her, Jiji was grumbling, "Wearing this wool thing on top of perfectly fine fur, I'll turn into a 'sheep cat' . . . but you can't refuse when a sweet, old lady like that gives you something."

But Kiki could see that Jiji was not altogether displeased with the band's lovely colors. When she told him, "It really suits you well," Jiji said, "So, does this make me look 'far out' enough for you?"

At the spot where the Big River flowed into the ocean, there was a harbor. There were two large passenger boats tied up at the pier and another just being pulled in by a tugboat. All around them, a flotilla of small boats was moving up and down. The sounds of steam whistles echoed back and forth across the water. Far off in the distance on the lefthand side was Morimo Point. From way up in the sky, everything below seemed to be moving very slowly and sluggishly.

Kiki paused in midair several times to search the water below her for a vessel with the name *Te-te* written on its side. First, she checked to be sure the boat was not in the port, and then she went on, scanning the ocean beyond. As she moved out of the harbor, the wind from below suddenly blew stronger. The number of vessels on the water grew fewer and were scattered far and wide. Then, far in the distance, Kiki caught sight of what looked like a tum-tum streamer. It was like a tiny white petal floating on the deep blue water. As they drew closer, Kiki could hear that the sound coming out of the smokestack along with the smoke sounded very tired and lackluster. Could that sound, as old Granny had said, be the sound of yawning? On the side of the boat, through the flaking, faded paint, the name *Te-te* was barely visible.

Kiki called out from above, "To the captain of the *Te-te*: You have a delivery, sir!"

The ship hands, clutching protectively at a cluster of large jugs sitting on the deck, all gaped up at her in surprise.

"I'm the Witch's Express. May I come down?"

"Please do, please do!"

The captain stuck his head out of the pilothouse and waved at her. And then, suddenly, lowering his voice, he said, "But please come down very gently, so as not to surprise our cargo."

"What, I heard you were carrying wine! Is it really some kind of animal?"

Kiki, too, kept her voice low as she alighted ever-so-gently on the deck.

The sailors were gathered around, completely agog at the girl who had suddenly dropped out of the sky. But the most surprised was Kiki herself. She had imagined that only the captain would be very fat, but now she found that all the men of the crew had great round bellies, like wealthy men who love to eat. They were just lucky, she thought to herself, that the ship didn't sink from the weight, but she stopped herself from smiling.

"Captain, this is from your mother. It's a nice, warm bellyband."

"What!? Good heavens, she never gives up . . ." wailed the captain. He sounded very irked, and even the members of the ship's crew were murmuring to each other with knowing looks, and saying things like, "This is really going too far."

"But this looks far too big to fit your stomach, Captain," said Kiki. "She said we could tuck it in, but still . . ." She spread out the immense bellyband, and the blue and white band looked even more lovely there on the deck of the ship riding on the waves.

"Hey, wait a minute!" exclaimed the captain, "This is not for me! It's for the ship's smokestack. You see," he began quickly to explain, "this is supposed to be a tum-tum steamer, but it's changed its tune these days. It sort of idles and yawns—sounds like it's short on sleep or something. So Granny decided it was because the smokestack had 'got a chill,' and she told me, 'The best medicine for a chill is a bellyband.' Ah, she can be pretty hard to get along with, I tell you!"

"Huh!? You say this bellyband is for the smokestack . . .?" For a moment, Kiki was speechless. She gazed up at the large smokestack. Yes, the bellyband she had carried certainly looked as if it would fit exactly.

"That old Granny," said the exasperated captain, "she won't be happy until everything in the whole world has a bellyband. It's too much. Just look, will you. I'm doing my best to do as she says, but it's really going too far."

The captain, fumbling with his buttons, finally got his coat open, and showed Kiki layer upon layer of bellybands, snugly encircling his belly in colorful rings.

"Even us," came a chorus from the ship's crew, lifting up their shirts. "We can barely move, all trussed up like this." The bellies of each and every one were clasped in colorful concentric layers of bellybands. What Kiki had mistaken for big-eaters' bellies were, in fact, bellyband bellies. Kiki leaned over, shaking with laughter.

Then one of the crewmen said hesitantly, "Captain, sir. Who is this person . . .?"

"This is the girl who runs the Witch's Express we hear so much about in town. Aren't you?" he addressed Kiki.

"Yes," nodded Kiki, trying to control her giggles.

"Say, Captain, why don't you ask her to do us a favor. They say she'll carry anything. If she'd pick up this whole ship and carry it through the air, we wouldn't have to worry about these rough waves."

"What?! Wait a minute!" Kiki caught her breath in surprise. "The whole ship! I couldn't possibly. But why?" she demanded.

"It's all because of the cargo, you see," said the captain.

"We've got a load of high-quality wine, and we're supposed to move it gently, without any jiggling . . . And, well, I thought since we weren't going all that great a distance, we could just keep the bottles here on the deck. But that turned out to be a mistake; the bottles keep hitting each other. If we go on like this, the wine will be ruined. So I've got everybody out here, trying to keep the bottles from jiggling too much, but it's hard work. "

Kiki could see how the bottles were simply set out on deck, and when the ship rolled and they knocked into each other, froth began to form on the surface of the wine inside.

"Why don't you set all the bottles apart?"

"If we did that, they'd start falling over. Are you sure you can't just carry the ship through the air?"

Kiki was sure, but she was also in a pickle. She began to glance frantically around the ship, looking for a solution. The sign she had hung up when she opened for business *did* say that she would carry anything. If that was what she promised, she couldn't afford to break her word. But a *ship*—even a tired-out tum-tum steamer—was a ship, not something little Kiki could just sling over her shoulder and fly off in the air with. Then she had an idea.

"Would it help if the bottles didn't jiggle against each other?" she asked. She was looking back and forth, from the bellyband-ballooning waists of the crewmen to the broad-bellied bottles of wine.

"Yes! That's what we have to do. It should be very simple, but it's very hard to manage up here on the deck."

"If that's true," said Kiki, "I think there's a very simple solution. In fact, we can solve two problems at once."

"What do you mean? Tell us, tell us!" The captain and all the crew members were eager to hear her idea.

"How important is it that you mind what your mother says?" Kiki asked the captain. "Do you think she would forgive you this once?"

The captain grinned and shrugged with a gesture that meant he'd bet she would.

"In that case," said Kiki, "you should all take off your bellybands and put them on the bottles. That will take the load off all your stomachs and make it easier to work, and the bottles will all be well padded and the wine won't be spoiled."

"Wow! That's a great idea. That makes sense!"

The captain quickly began to take off his bellybands, pushing them down to his legs and stepping out of them, one by one. In no time, he was down to his own, quite normal proportions. The crewmen, too, rapidly shed their bellybands, which piled up into a colorful mountain on the deck, revealing a lineup of slender, solid-bodied seamen.

Then they all set to putting the bellybands gently around the wine bottles. When they were finished, it was the bottles that looked like they had rich-men's paunches in the colorful bands, and they sat snugly together, with no sound of jiggling or jostling.

"It works!" The captain and the crew all smiled with relief and satisfaction.

"Well, then I think I'll be going," said Kiki to the captain, starting to get astride her broom with Jiji, and then she remembered, "Oh! I almost forgot. This bellyband for the smokestack. Don't you think it would be a good idea to mind Granny at least on this one?"

"Okay, I guess we should." The captain assented reluctantly, for he was obviously greatly relieved about the wine. The crewmen also nodded in agreement. Then they all worked together to put the great sky-blue and white bellyband around the smokestack. Kiki saw the job done and then said, "All right, now I really will be going." As they flew away, Kiki waved gaily at the crew of the *Te-te*. And then she pointed the broomstick back toward the city of Koriko. Behind her, she could hear the sound of the ship's engine fading in the distance. It might have been her imagination, but it seemed to her that the sound had changed from the tired-out sound Granny had so worried about to the regular tum-tum, tum-tum of a healthy steamship.

The next day, Kiki was astounded to read in the newspaper the news that the crew of the *Te-te* had all been afflicted with stomach flu. And then, down below that, there was a small article that said:

A liquor store on Morimo Point has
started to sell bottles of wine wrapped
in colorful knit bands. The flavor is fine,
the shape is fine, the price is rather high,
but it's an excellent buy for the money.

A week passed, and Jiji showed no sign of taking off the bellyband Granny had slipped over him. Quite the contrary, he seemed to be taking care of it, dusting it off now and then with whisks of his tail. For Jiji himself had overheard a remark while he was out on a walk in the town: "See, the witch's cat is different; he's keeping his magic warm."

Another week later, a message came to Kiki from Granny that Kiki's own bellyband was finished. When Kiki went to pick it up, she found it was a beautiful mixture of pastel colors, like a bottle of sugar candies. Granny said, "There you are, dear. I know you have to wear black on the outside all the time, but at least you can enjoy the bright colors of your bellyband underneath, where it doesn't show." And Kiki could not help but ask her one more favor.

"Granny, would you please teach me how to knit? I want to learn how to do many things."

"Oh! I'd be happy to. And what are you going to knit, my girl?" she asked, with a sly twinkle in her eye.

Kiki started to say, "For my mother and father . . ."

But Granny finished her sentence for her, without hesitation: ". . . bellybands, of course."

Chapter 9
Kiki Rings in the New Year

It was New Year's Eve in the city of Koriko. In only four hours, the old year would be over. In every house in the city, people had finished their preparations for the new year. Windows were shining clean and the warm, orange glow of people's homes spilled out into the streets.

Kiki was feeling lonely. Ever since she was born, she had enjoyed the happiness and pleasures of this season at home with her father, her mother, and her cat, Jiji. This year, there was only Jiji to keep her company. A girl witch who had left home on her maiden journey could not go home for one whole year, not even at New Year's.

Well, Kiki was thinking to herself, I have only four months to go. I may as well enjoy the time as much as I can. I've got to make the best of it; I can't give up now.

Kiki decided to put lonely thoughts out of her mind and began to make meatballs. In the town where Kiki was born, it was the custom to eat meatballs stewed in tomato sauce on New Year's Eve. Everyone would sit around eating meatballs and recalling the things that had happened during the past year. And, when at last the clock would strike twelve, everyone would hug the person next to them and exclaim, "Hail the old year, hail the new year!"

Her meatballs were as big as apples. Trying her best to recall how her mother made them, she stewed them in preserved tomatoes she had canned during the summer. Sprinkling salt and pepper in the pot, Kiki said to Jiji, "I guess it's just going to be you and me this year, Jiji, so let's have our meatballs, and when it gets to be twelve o'clock, let's do our salutations, just like always, okay?"

Jiji put both paws out in front of him and stretched long and slow. "Oh, sure, why not. If nothing happens between now and then, I guess we can call it a good year. In fact, depending on how you look at it, we haven't had a bad year, all in all."

But there's something very strange about the town tonight, thought Kiki as she stirred the soup and checked the seasoning. Even though it was New Year's, when she thought that people would be celebrating together in their own separate homes, it seemed that people were gathering out in the streets instead.

And then came a call at the door, and the sound of Osono's voice yelling, "Hello there!" The baker's wife came in, carrying her baby. The baby had grown quite big and was waving its legs. Osono came up to Kiki and said, in a formal tone quite unlike her usual greeting, "Don't forget to listen!"

The way she said it made Kiki suspect, again, that there was something strange going on.

"But listen for what, for heaven's sake, and why?"

Then it was Osono's turn to look mystified, but she soon saw why Kiki was puzzled.

"Oh, that's right!" Osono exclaimed. "This is your first New Year's Eve in this town. I completely forgot. I should have told you about our New Year's Eve greetings. Now, come here and look."

Osono was pointing out the window to the clock tower, stretching high up over the buildings of the town.

"See that clock? Even if you want to know the time, it's usually hidden in the clouds, and when it isn't, it's so high you get a crick in your neck trying to see the clock face. But, once a year, that clock plays a very important role in this town. And that's on New Year's Eve. On New Year's Eve that clock tolls only the hour of twelve midnight. The bell rings twelve times, and the twelfth ring signals the start of a marathon. All the people of the town run in it. They start in front of the city hall and circle through the whole city. You know, it's like *running* into the New Year. This is a very important event in this town and it has been celebrated, without fail, ever since that clock tower was built. And, so as we won't forget to listen for the tolling of the midnight bells, somehow the custom arose of greeting each other on New Year's Eve with the words, 'Don't forget to listen.'"

"So is that why there are so many people out in the town?"

"Yes. Of course. The eager beavers are out there early, greeting everyone they meet and waiting for midnight when the marathon starts."

"Oh, so that's what's going on. Can I run in the marathon too?" Kiki said eagerly.

"Of course you can! But," said Osono, with a twinkle in her eye, "you can't fly. That wouldn't be fair."

"Oh, I wouldn't do that!" laughed Kiki.

"I'm going to run with my husband this year, and take the baby on my back, and you must come along, too," said Osono, going back to the house.

Kiki picked up her long skirts and began to run in place to warm up for the marathon. Jiji, too, began to shake out one leg at a time, the look of a serious runner on his face.

About two hours later, the young mayor of the city of Koriko was sitting in front of his desk in city hall. Finally, all the work he had to do before the end of the year was finished, and he stretched with a great sigh of relief. Everything he had done since he had been elected mayor at the beginning of the year had gone well. People seemed pleased with him, saying he was doing a good job for one so young. And tonight, at the end of such a successful year, the mayor was in the best of spirits and raring to go. He was determined to run at the head of the traditional New Year's marathon to show the people of the town that, even more than ever, he was the man they could rely on to lead them.

The mayor stretched his arms and shook out his leg muscles, readying himself for the race. Then he opened the window of his office. Looking out over the town, he shouted out as loud as he could the New Year's Eve greeting, "Don't forget to listen!"

And then he realized that something was wrong, and it so astounded him that he nearly lost his grip on the window frame. The mayor's office was on the top floor of city hall so, when the window was open, he could always hear the ticking of the clock far, far overhead, even if it was shrouded in clouds and even if it was raining hard. But now, to his amazement and alarm, the sound that came from the clock was not its usual brisk ticking, but a dull and listless thunking.

The mayor stuck his head out of the window as far as he could and peered up at the clock. As he did so, the clock emitted a few final, faint strokes and then, as if relieved that the mayor had noticed its fateful state, it stopped. The time was 10:36. There was only an hour and 24 minutes left before 12:00, when the clock had its most important task of the entire year to perform.

The mayor leapt to the phone and called the clock maker who, as his forebears had been, was in charge of maintenance and repairs of the clock.

"The tower clock has stopped! Get over here as fast as you can. And don't you dare tell a soul!"

After putting down the receiver, the mayor himself hurried to climb up the clock tower. The clock had not broken down once, ever since it had been installed, so the annual New Year's marathon had always started punctually on the stroke of midnight. The clock and its role at New Year's were the boast of the town. Nothing could be more inopportune than for the clock to stop now, on this crucial night of his first year as mayor. How awful to think that such a happening might be inscribed in the annals of the town's history! His reputation would be ruined. The young and energetic mayor was determined, at all costs, to avoid such a dishonor.

It wasn't long until the clock maker came puffing up the 2,358 steps of the clock tower with his great tool bag. The clock maker had—like his father and grandfathers before him, going back at least five generations—taken the best of care of the great town clock and the clock had never once been out of order in all its long history. But now . . . The clock maker's heart began to pound as rapidly as the clock had when it was at its fittest. Could it have been that just last week, when he came to set the clock for the last time in preparation for this very important event, he'd done something wrong?

Pale with apprehension, the clock maker went to work. Tapping with a small hammer, he checked the screws and the wheels of the clockworks. The largest wheel in the mechanism turned out to be broken. The clock maker was relieved. At least it wasn't his fault.

"I found out what's wrong," he announced to the mayor. "It's just the main wheel in the clockworks. It's broken. It's simple enough, though, so we'll just replace it. The job will be done in three minutes."

"Are you sure?" The mayor unconsciously went back to his warming-up exercises, but then asked again, "Are you sure? And can you correct the time, too?"

"Yes," the clock maker reassured him, "as soon as we have a new main wheel, it can be done in no time."

"Are you sure it will ring twelve o'clock like it's supposed to?"

"Of course it will." The clock maker's fears had completely vanished; he sounded full of confidence. He even began to whistle a tune as he peered into his great tool bag. Then, suddenly, his face went white as a sheet again, and his hands began to tremble.

"But, but," he stuttered, looking helplessly at the mayor, "I don't have a replacement wheel."

"What! Well, for heaven's sake, go and get it . . . right away!" The mayor, too, turned pale again.

"But the fact is, there isn't one. Not even in my shop. We'll have to order it made."

"Well, hurry! Hurry!" screeched the mayor, desperately.

"But it would take fifty-three days!" said the clock maker.

The mayor reeled backwards as if he had been struck, and then he said, with a painful groan, "Isn't there a replacement anywhere?"

"Well, actually, there is another wheel just like this, but it's . . . it wouldn't be easy to get at."

"Come on, tell me!" demanded the mayor impatiently.

"Well, you know the town on the other side of the three mountains to the west? I've heard it has a clock just like this one. If we could . . . sort of . . . borrow its main wheel . . ."

"Borrow its wheel?"

"Yes, you know, sort of without telling anybody . . ."

"You mean, *steal* it?"

"Yes, but . . ."

"What do you mean, 'but.'"

"We're not thieves."

"I don't care. You go and get it yourself," demanded the mayor.

"Who? Me? Well, yes, I could. But . . . there's no time. Well, if I could use a police car with a siren, maybe I could get there and get back on time . . ."

"Don't be silly! Do you think you're going to use a police car to go and *steal* something?! Isn't there some other way?"

"Well, gee . . . Oh, yes! There might be a way," the clock maker's face lighted up. "You know, in this town there's a witch . . ."

The telephone in Kiki's office began to ring. Kiki had just finished eating her meatballs, which had turned out to be quite delicious, and was warming up for the marathon. Picking up the receiver, she did a small curtsey and sang cheerfully into the phone the evening's greeting, "Don't forget to listen!"

But the voice on the other end snapped back sharply, "Forget about 'not forgetting to listen.' I'm the mayor of this town. Now, I hear that you are in the business of delivering things. Could we get you to go and get something?"

"Now there's no need to get irritated," said Kiki calmly and coolly. "My business is delivering things and, of course, I'll be happy to deliver something either from here to there or from there to here."

"Good! I'm glad to hear that. In that case, I'd like you to come over to the great clock tower right away. Please come as fast as you can," he added in a slightly more courteous tone.

With Jiji behind her, Kiki took off on her broom toward the clock tower. But she was feeling very put out. Tonight of all nights, she had not wanted to be flying off on other people's errands. She had wanted to be running the marathon down there on the ground, with everybody else. Looking down, she could see many people gathered in front of city hall, waiting for the clock to toll midnight.

When she arrived at the clock tower, the mayor got right down to business.

"Now, here's what we'd like you to do. As it happens, the big main wheel of the works in this clock is broken. We'd like you to go

over the three mountains to the west, to the town over there, and
. . . pinch the . . ." The mayor swallowed his words, ". . . with super-
express speed. Now, you'll do it, right? You'll do it?"

"What do you mean, 'pinch'?" Kiki's eyes grew round with
astonishment.

Now the mayor hunched secretively and said in a whisper, "I
mean we want to just 'borrow' the big main wheel from the clock in
that town, just long enough to make this clock strike twelve. That's
all."

"You mean *steal* the wheel?" demanded Kiki.

"Shh! Don't say it like that. A nice little girl like you shouldn't
use a word like that. No, we're just going to borrow it. And we're
going to return it immediately."

"If that's all you have to do, why don't you just ring the bell by
hand? The clock's so high up, people can't see what time it says
anyway."

But the clock maker shook his head apologetically. "Because of the
way this clock is made, it won't ring unless the hands move until the
two come together at 12. I'm sorry to say . . . that's the way it is."

Kiki tried again. "Well, then, when it's 12:00, Mr. Mayor, all
you'll have to do is start the race yourself with a hand signal or
something!"

"No, it's no good." The mayor shook his head vigorously. "A
custom that has been practiced for such a long time isn't something
you just change that easily. Why, if we did something like that—you
never know, people might sprain their ankles or break out in rashes,
or goodness knows what . . ." He sounded desperate. "Now come on,
won't you just go and get that wheel? We just don't have any time
left."

The mayor was in such a tizzy, his face was going red with
embarrassment and white with apprehension by turns. The deep
furrow in his brow made his eyebrows slant steeply upwards. He
looked as if he had been crying as he gazed pleadingly at Kiki.

Kiki realized that he wasn't going to budge. She couldn't just say no, but she definitely did not like to be asked to steal something, so she set her lips and took off without answering clearly, one way or the other.

To the west of the city of Koriko were three mountains, lined up primly in a row, and beyond them were the lights of a town shining like a crystal necklace laid out along the valley.

"Hey, Kiki," called Jiji, clutching Kiki's back as she flew along, "can you really do it without getting caught?"

"I won't know until I get there and see. Maybe we can explain the circumstances, and they might loan us the big wheel just for a little while," said Kiki, mostly to reassure herself.

The town turned out to be small and they quickly located the clock tower. Kiki made herself very tiny and inconspicuous as she landed at the top of the tower, but the sight below caught her by surprise. The square before the clock tower was filled with people, just as it was in Koriko, and now and then they would glance up at the clock, obviously as conscious of the time as the people in the city from which she had come. Kiki quietly moved down to the ground, keeping out of sight in the shadow of the rooftops. People were chatting animatedly, and Kiki noticed that, as they talked, they were sticking out the little fingers of their right hands and moving them up and down, up and down, as if doing little-finger exercises.

Do you suppose that the new year starts out in this town, not with a marathon, but with pinky-finger calisthenics? thought Kiki to herself. Just then, an old man sang out beside her, "Don't forget twelve o'clock."

That gave Kiki another start. The way he said it was exactly the way the people of Koriko said, "Don't forget to listen!"

So Kiki asked the man, "Excuse me, but could you tell me what this gathering is?"

"What! You mean you don't know?" the old man said with amazement. "When twelve o'clock comes around, people greet each other with 'Let's be friends in the coming year too,' and they link their little fingers in promise with the people next to them. It's been the custom since long, long ago in this town."

The old man smiled broadly and held out his own little finger toward Kiki.

"Look, it's almost time!" he said cheerfully, "are you ready? Gracious sakes! What are you doing holding a broom? Haven't you finished your cleaning yet? Better hurry up!"

The old man prodded her to hurry. Caught off balance for a moment, Kiki found her way out of the crowd and hastily said to Jiji, "Well, let's get back!"

"But what are you going to do about the clock's wheel?" said Jiji worriedly, looking up at Kiki.

"We'll forget about it. Let's get going," said Kiki.

"But . . . but, you know, we were just going to 'borrow' it for a little while. You mean you're not going to take it?"

"That's right. I can't do any such thing. Just look. If I were to 'borrow' the wheel, even for a 'little while,' that clock wouldn't strike twelve. And then all the people of this town would miss the moment to renew their promises of friendship for the new year. Why, that might mean that people wouldn't get along in this town next year."

"But what about Koriko? What are you going to do about its clock?"

"I'm thinking about it." From the shadow of a building, Kiki took off speedily into the night sky.

When Kiki got back to the clock tower in Koriko, the mayor and the clock maker rushed up to her.

"Well, where's the clock's wheel?"

Kiki held out her empty hands. "I don't have it. But you don't have to worry. I'm going to take care of things. Now, both of you can go on down and wait in the square. Just leave it to me."

"But . . ." Looking distraught, neither man looked about to move from his spot.

"It'll be all right. Remember, I'm a witch. I'll take care of it," said Kiki briskly, urging the two toward the stairs. Then, when they were gone, she spread her arms wide, and took a deep breath.

"All right, Jiji, now you've got to help me. I want you to hang on tight and push from behind with all your might."

Her face set with intense concentration, Kiki climbed onto her broom. Rocketing off from the tower, Kiki sped off over to the edge of the city, deftly banked right, and, picking up speed, headed straight back toward the clock tower. Then, just as she was about to collide with the clock, she grasped its long hand with both hands, circled above the clock's face, and rotated the hand one full turn plus 24 minutes until the two hands came together at twelve.

"Bong, bong, bong . . ."

From high above, the clock's bell rang out over the city. And then, from the square in front of the city hall below, a swelling cry arose, and the sound of running feet began to echo through the town as the marathon began.

Kiki, who had let go of the clock's long hand, was flung right out to the edge of the city again on the momentum of the broom's flight. When finally she was able to get the broom under control again, she made her way back to the clock tower and plunked down, exhausted. Her hair was disheveled and she felt as if the insides of her head had shifted to one side. Shaking her head to get things back in place, she peered down into the square. At the very head of all the runners, making himself conspicuous with great strides, was the mayor.

"Wow! That was really something!" said Jiji, lying stretched out on the tower, flat, as flat as a pancake, "I thought my tail was going to be blown away."

"Me, too. I thought I might have my whole face scraped off."

With a sigh of relief, Kiki took a look at her wristwatch. But, to her dismay, it was still five minutes *before* 12:00. Kiki began to giggle, and then to laugh out loud.

"I guess we sort of did it *too* fast! Well, maybe better early than late. Anyway, it's done." She made a face, sticking out her tongue clownishly.

"There you go again, careless as ever . . ." remarked Jiji. And then suddenly he shouted, "Oh, no! It's gone . . . My tummy warmer, it's gone!"

"Well, so it is. It must have peeled off in our blast. But you don't really need it anyway, do you?"

"Yes I do! I really liked that tummy warmer, and besides, without it, you know, I'll just go back to being an ordinary black cat. Gee, we didn't even get a token of thanks, and I lost big this time."

Hoping to comfort Jiji, Kiki said, "But just think, Jiji, it was you and me who rang in the new year. Have you ever heard of such a delivery service in your life? The New Year's bell tolled because of what you and I did. Is that something just any old black cat can do? Now think about that, and let's go and run with everybody else. We'll go and catch up with them on the broom. It'll be fudging just a little bit, but then we can run with Osono and the baker. Let's look for Tombo and Mimi, too, okay? Come, let's go!"

Snatching up Jiji, Kiki leapt upon her broom and off they went.

After that New Year's Eve, even people she didn't know often greeted Kiki in the town, and Kiki thought happily to herself that the new year had given people a new lease on life. But then, one day, Osono told her why everyone was suddenly so nice to her.

"The clock maker has been telling everyone about what you did. He told them how you fixed the broken clock wheel in time to make the clock ring 12:00, and he's saying a witch that can do magic like that is what every town needs. It makes me feel really good, you know. After all, that's what I thought from the beginning!"

Chapter 10
Kiki Carries the Sounds of Spring

It was a long, cold winter. Jiji huddled on a chair, grumbling.

"When is it ever going to get warm again? If it keeps up like this, I may give up being a cat. I can't stand it any longer."

"Oh? And what are you going to become instead?" inquired Kiki, giving Jiji a sharp tap on the back. "What's wrong with that lovely fur coat you have? You keep complaining how cold it is, but the sound of the wind has changed, you know. It's the sound of spring, I'm sure. Spring! When we can go back home to Mother! But I guess creatures like you are too busy complaining to hear such lovely sounds."

Jiji gave her a doleful look and curled up tighter, covering his face with his front paws. But his little black ears were twitching ever so slightly this way and that, listening for the whispers of spring.

"Ding a-ling, Ding a-ling."

The telephone rang, and an urgent voice leapt out at Kiki as she picked up the receiver.

"Hello . . . Please, please come and help us. As fast as you can! Could you please come to the train station? It's Koriko Central Station. Please come quickly!" And then the receiver clicked on the other end of the line.

"Goodness!" said Kiki, as she scurried around getting ready to go, "Why is it that all the people who ask us for help these days are in such a hurry!"

As Kiki and Jiji flew over Central Station, they could see the stationmaster on the platform waving to them. "Here we are. Over here. Please hurry!" he yelled. Beside him stood a group of eight men, all as skinny as rails, and all wearing matching black suits. Even when Kiki came down out of the sky in front of them on her broom, they showed not the slightest sign of surprise, but continued to glare fearsomely at the stationmaster.

The stationmaster began to explain the situation to Kiki, saying "These gentlemen are musical performers . . . ," but one of the men interrupted him sharply with, "We are *not* 'musical performers.' We are musicians!"

"Oh, yes. That's right," said the stationmaster. "Now, these musicians are scheduled to present a concert at the Outdoor Concert Hall this afternoon . . . "

"What! When it's so cold?" said Kiki with surprise. "You mean a concert outside?"

The man speaking for the musicians cleared his throat haughtily and drew up his chest proudly. "We are doing this concert precisely because it is cold. Our concert, in fact, will warm the cockles of your heart. We've even named the performance 'Concert Heralding the Coming of Spring.' Well, that's what we intend," he said with a sour look. "Whether or not the people of this town will have an ear for such music . . . I'm beginning to have my doubts. Some of you seem quite hopeless."

"Unfortunately," sighed the stationmaster. "Now, Miss Delivery Service, what happened is that these musicians' instruments were

not unloaded from the train they were traveling on. It's terrible. It's a travesty. We don't know what to do."

The stationmaster took off his cap and used it to wipe the sweat from his brow. A few steps away, Kiki could see two young porters standing off to the side, looking abashed and ashamed.

"Well!"

Kiki floated the broom off the ground a little, to get a look in the direction the train had gone.

"So, that's what happened. The train left with the instruments still on board," finished the stationmaster.

"Then I'd guess you'd better quickly telephone the next station and tell them the problem. And then I'll go and pick up the instruments there."

"But you see, the train was an express train, and it doesn't stop anywhere until the very end of the line."

The stationmaster was looking more and more uncomfortable.

"All right, then, what is it that you would like me to do?" inquired Kiki, nonplussed.

"We were thinking . . . maybe, you could catch up with the train and get in through a window . . . Oh, no, I suppose that wouldn't work . . . They're in the last car of the train, by the way."

"Oh! That's impossible. How could I do that?" Kiki's voice rose in astonishment.

"But it *has* been done. There are people who've crawled in the train windows and stolen gold bars and such. "

"I've never heard of anything so . . . !" Kiki could hardly believe her ears. She had to think of a better solution.

"Wouldn't it be better to just borrow some instruments? Certainly you could find the appropriate instruments somewhere in this city."

"Well, we considered that, but . . . " said the stationmaster, glancing nervously at the black-suited men.

"Impossible!" said one, in a thunderous voice. "Unthinkable!

We're not the kind of musicians who play just any old music on just any old instruments. Not us! How could we possibly play on plain, old instruments that will sound at the least breath of air!" And all the other seven men standing in the row nodded emphatically, their eyebrows raised even higher than before.

"Humph," mumbled Kiki under her breath. "How could these fellows, who look as cold and sharp as the North Wind itself, ever perform a concert heralding the spring? I have my doubts." Jiji, the only one who could hear her, whispered agreement in her ear, adding, "But watch out—that's an insult to the North Wind!"

"All this trouble because you didn't have our instruments unloaded," the man who had spoken first was repeating to the stationmaster.

"We labeled them clearly as 'Bound for Koriko' so there's no fault on our part. The entire responsibility is yours, Mr. Stationmaster!"

The stationmaster looked desperately at Kiki for help. And the two porters, too, fixed her with pleading eyes. Kiki shrugged her shoulders and threw up her hands. When people asked her like that, she just couldn't refuse.

"Well, I don't know whether I can get them back, but at least I can try to catch up with the train and see."

"Well, hurry!" ordered the man speaking for the musicians, in an authoritative tone. "And, remember, there isn't much time left. We'll be waiting at the Outdoor Concert Hall, so be sure to bring them by 3:00. Have you got that?"

Kiki found his imperious manner unbearable, but instead of retorting, she simply took off immediately, without even answering him.

Kiki flew straight up, high into the sky, and then began to follow the train tracks through the landscape below. The tracks stretched northward through the city, passed fields and forests, and then entered the mountains, threading through one tunnel after another.

"Hey! Do you really think you can pull off such a trick?" asked Jiji anxiously from the rear.

"Sure, I can do it. But that fellow was so pompous, I couldn't help being a little mean."

"But how are we going to get onto a train that's moving?"

"You're with me aren't you? It'll be all right."

"What do you mean?" screeched Jiji.

"There! Look! There it is!" Kiki raised herself up on the broom to get a better look. The last car of the train was just disappearing, like the tail of a lizard, into a tunnel. Gathering momentum with a loud cry, Kiki flew steeply up over the mountain and circled around to the other end of the tunnel.

"They said their instruments were in the very last car, so we'll land on its roof. Then, Jiji, I want you to get in one of the windows, and open the door at the back of the car. Okay?"

It wasn't long before the train appeared out of the tunnel, sounding its whistle. Kiki pointed her broomstick downward and made ready for her descent.

"How are you going to land on such a small space?" Jiji looked terrified. And even Kiki was beginning to feel very scared of this attempt to land on top of a moving train, as it sped along like a flying leaf. Kiki was thinking to herself that, if only she knew a spell that would stop this train, this job would be as easy as pie. How frustrating to be a witch with such limited powers!

"Well, I guess we don't have much choice. Here goes!"

Kiki put aside her fears and began the descent toward the train. The wind roared in her ears and through her hair, and Jiji's fur stood on end.

"Watch out! We'll hit!" screamed Jiji. And Kiki slid the broom along her body and caught hold of the top of the train. The train rolled on, oblivious. Sliding along the rollicking roof, Kiki made her way to a window that was partly open and peered inside.

There they were. The pile with a sign saying "Bound for Koriko" had to be the instruments.

"All right, Jiji. In you go!" commanded Kiki.

"No! No! I can't! I'll fall!"

Jiji kept backing up, refusing to let go of the broomstick.

"Come on. You'll be all right. Now, go!" Kiki took Jiji by the scruff of the neck and pushed him in through the window.

Branches of the trees along the train tracks stuck out, whipping Kiki as the train passed. Every time she would crouch down along the roof to avoid one bunch of branches, the next bunch would rush toward her.

"Jiji! Hurry up! Open the door! Hurry, please!" Kiki hung out over the backdoor, banging her fist on the train.

Then suddenly the train entered another tunnel. It was pitch black and, with a tremendous roar, the wind swooshed over the train from one end. Kiki's body slid along the roof until she thought she was going to fall off. Frantically grasping her broom, Kiki managed to catch hold, but then her body fell halfway off the roof.

"Jiji, Jiji!" she screamed, kicking the side of the train with her feet. Then suddenly, the door opened and Kiki dropped down into the car. At the same moment, the train came out of the tunnel. Bright light streamed in through the window. Looking stunned, Jiji was sitting on his haunches on the floor, gazing at her blankly.

There was a huge pile of luggage left on the train, but Kiki found the instruments quickly because they were all in odd-shaped cases. When she had identified them all, she realized what a tremendous load they made.

"How am I ever going to carry all these things?" Kiki wailed, plunking herself down hopelessly.

"Look. All the cases have these grips and handles," said Jiji, whose spirits had finally revived. Rubbing himself against Kiki's legs, he suggested "Maybe you could string them on the broomstick."

"All eight of them? I wonder . . .?"

"Looks like it might be pretty difficult."

"Oh! Wait a minute," said Kiki. "I bet they'd be a lot lighter if we took them out of these cases.

Kiki opened the case nearest to her. Inside was a gleaming brass horn. The shape reminded her of the spiral slide at the amusement park.

"Look," said Kiki, "here's a trumpet. And there. And there's another. Here's a violin . . . and a cello." Kiki opened all the cases, one by one, and, as one might expect from musicians who took such immense pride in their profession, every instrument had been polished to a dazzling shine.

"Jiji, you could manage to carry at least the violin? I'll hold the cello, and we'll tie together all these horns on a rope in order of size and carry them along that way. We'll just make use of some of the rope from the luggage here."

Chattering busily, Kiki deftly knotted the instruments, one at a time, along the rope and tied one end firmly to the broomstick.

"All right, Jiji. Let's get going! Get on behind."

She got on the broom, gripping the cello with her left hand and steadying it with her knees, and holding the bow in her right hand. Jiji clutched the violin, which was actually bigger than he was, with four paws and wrapped his tail around the broom whisk to steady himself.

"Here we go!" shouted Kiki, and they took off through the open door of the train, the instruments trailing behind them. As they rose into the air, the wind began to whistle through the trumpets and trombones, with each blaring out a different tune. The passengers in the train began sticking their heads out of the windows, pointing and exclaiming with astonishment at the sight of the instruments flying through the air.

Seeing their surprise, Kiki told them, "You never know what can happen in the skies," and then she exclaimed to herself, "Isn't this a beautiful cello?"

Entranced by the instrument she was holding, Kiki set the bow to the strings and began to play. Jiji plucked the strings of the violin with his claws. Neither of them had ever touched such instruments before so, at first, the sounds that they made were squeaky and off-key—the kind of noise that makes your teeth rattle and your hair stand on end. The trumpets and other brass instruments, too, sounded a capricious cacophony of wheezes, boops, bleeps, and snores.

But then a warm south wind swept up, and began to whistle through the instruments, making them resonate with soft and gentle tones. Delighted with the accidental music they were making, Kiki began to experiment, trying out the sounds she could produce by steering the broom in wide curves to the right and then the left, or by pointing the broom in steep ascent or descent. Little by little, they approached the city of Koriko.

Meanwhile, back at the Outdoor Concert Hall in Koriko, the audience had gathered for the performance. It was already ten minutes past the appointed hour for the concert to begin. Over the center of the stage was a banner that read "Concert Heralding the Coming of Spring" and below it sat the eight sour-looking musicians, facing the audience. While they looked very cool and calm on the outside, inside they were in a torment of worry over whether Kiki would really return with their precious instruments. Standing backstage, in even more of a fret, were the stationmaster and the young porters.

The audience began to grow impatient, "Hey, it's cold. Let's get started!"

Then someone added sarcastically, "We're going to freeze to death out here. Weren't you going to bring the spring with you?" The crowd began to whistle and jeer at the musicians.

Finally, one of the musicians got up and spoke. "We'll begin quite soon. Now please, everyone, may I invite you to wait patiently. Even beneath these cold skies, once we put our hands to our instruments, the sounds you will hear will bring forth the spring in your hearts. At this moment, we are engaged in preparatory prayers for this performance."

The musician cast his gaze slowly over the crowd, and cleared his throat commandingly.

The other musicians, sitting in their row, likewise hid their anxiety and impatience, cleared their throats, and gazed at the ground as if absorbed in prayer. Chastened by the musician's words, the members of the audience, too, grew quiet and subdued.

And then, faintly at first, from somewhere, the air began to fill with an odd assortment of sounds:

Thwang, thwa-wa-an, thwang-ang-ang

Boogh, boo-oop-oop, bo-la-lang-lang

Iyan, iya-aa-an, iya-ang, lang.

The sounds seemed to flow from among the clouds, to reverberate from the hills, to lilt over the Big River and resonate off the ocean, murmuring and beguiling, like whispered secrets, as if the spring had indeed come in answer to all their prayers. The members of the audience and even the musicians themselves began to raise their heads and gaze about, craning their necks to see where the sounds were coming from. Then they saw in the distance that there was something bobbing up and down in the sky, gleaming brightly in the reflected rays of the afternoon sun. It approached very slowly, swooping broadly to the right and then to the left.

Thwang, thwa-wa-an, thwang-ang-ang

Chi-li-li, chi-li-li

Boogh, boo-oop-oop, bo-la-lang-lang

Pu-ri-ri, pu-ri-ri

Iyan, iya-aa-an, iya,ang, lang.

People who had been huddling in their winter coats with the collars turned up, and people who had been hunched over or who had pulled their feet up under them to keep warm, all began to stretch themselves out and gaze upward. As the sounds came closer, they all began to think about how much they wanted spring to come. But the most surprised of all were the musicians on the stage. They looked at each other and blinked with amazement, saying, "Hey! Who's making those sounds?"

Gradually, the glistening point of light grew clearer. It was Kiki and Jiji riding on the broom. What looked like a necklace of gleaming lights was the string of brass horns. The eight musicians rushed backstage, the sooner to collect their instruments from Kiki and begin the concert. The stationmaster and the young porters waved mightily, signaling Kiki to come down.

But Kiki acted as if she didn't even notice them. She was thoroughly enjoying plucking the strings of the cello, keeping time with the wind's performance on brass horns.

"Shall we keep flying a little longer?" asked Kiki, turning back to Jiji.

"Why not? Yes, let's," agreed Jiji serenely, as he clutched the violin. "After all, the train door might not have opened at all, so they can wait just a little longer."

The people below were surprised and impressed, "Yes, indeed, this is a wonderful concert."

"Who would ever have thought of having the music *blow in* from the sky . . ."

Some of them closed their eyes, drinking in the sounds. Others started waving. Some were tapping their feet. It put everyone in a springtime mood.

"I've got to start getting ready for spring."

"Say, I think I'll put violets on my bonnet this year."

And then the audience began to clap, and their applause welled larger and larger, until Kiki said, "All right, I'm going down now."

Kiki drew up the string of instruments into her lap so that they wouldn't be damaged by hitting the ground, and landed gently backstage where the musicians and the stationmaster were waiting.

As Kiki disappeared from sight behind the stage, the audience gave her one last wave of applause and then began to move out of their seats.

Backstage, the musicians rushed at Kiki to get their instruments. "How could you be so slow!" they complained, hurriedly detaching their instruments from the rope.

"It was the wind, you see . . ." Kiki said calmly, watching the musicians rush out onto the stage.

By the time they got there, however, the people in the audience had turned their backs and were streaming toward the exits.

"Wait, wait!" called one of the performers after them. One member of the audience turned back to say, "It was a wonderful concert. What a wonderful idea, to have that pretty little witch bring in the music from the skies. We hope you'll do it again."

Hearing these words, the mouths of all eight musicians dropped open in dismay and they moaned in disappointment.

When Kiki and Jiji took off again to fly back home, Jiji asked, "Say, Kiki, did you get any reward?"

"What are you talking about, after all the fun we got out of doing that job? What more were you expecting?" said Kiki, glancing back at her cat with surprise.

"I suppose you're right," nodded Jiji, and his black ears perked up sharply. "I can still hear the sounds of spring, you know."

"That's because it really *is* spring. That's the true sound of spring," said Kiki happily, gazing down over the city of Koriko.

"Just think," she said, "it's almost a whole year since we came to live here."

Chapter 11
Kiki Goes Home

Spring had indeed come to the city of Koriko. Kiki pulled a chair over to the sunshine at the window and sat gazing out, her knees pulled up under her chin. The slightly overcast sky emitted a soft light like the glow of a baby's cheeks.

"Day after tomorrow, it'll be one year. I can go home!" Kiki had been saying the same thing over and over.

Actually, Kiki found she was a little confused as the day approached. She felt a strange mixture of both excitement and apprehension.

"That's right. You've only got two days to go, today and tomorrow. Don't you have to get ready?" asked Jiji.

"Well, there's nothing that says we have to go home at exactly one year."

Listening to her, Jiji began to circle the room impatiently, thumping the floor with his tail.

"What's the matter with you, Kiki? We've been looking forward to this day for so long, and now that it's practically here, you don't seem excited at all!"

Staring at her knees, Kiki held up her skirts and pulled her knees to the side, where she could see her legs together.

"Say, Jiji, do you think I've changed at all? Do you suppose I've grown up a bit?"

"You've gotten taller, all right," said Jiji.

"Is that all?"

"Well, not all." Jiji fidgeted, wiggling his whiskers.

"Do you think I've succeeded—you know, in making a life of my own?" Kiki asked.

"What are you worrying about? After all this!" Jiji was feeling quite impatient with all Kiki's doubting. Then he looked at her and, cocking his head, said comfortingly, "Hey, you've done fine. I'd say you score top marks."

"Thank you," said Kiki, but she did not feel really satisfied with Jiji's praise, and fell back into a pensive mood.

Kiki had chosen to follow in her mother's footsteps, as any girl might have, and she had truly been on her own. She'd chosen the city of Koriko to settle down in by herself and she'd thought up the idea of a delivery business. Going back over all the things that had happened over the past year, there had been plenty of difficulties. And Kiki did think that she had done her best to cope with them.

Then why, she wondered, did she have such doubts? She had never thought she would be so uncertain. Back when she first left home, she was sure she would have been full of confidence, telling herself and everyone else, 'Look, I did it! I succeeded!'" without the least hesitation. But now, even after being told by Jiji that he gave her "top marks," she still couldn't be sure. She wanted to know for certain, and she knew she'd have to ask someone else.

"You're *not* going to tell me we're postponing our trip home," said Jiji, looking sideways at her.

"Oh, of course not!" answered Kiki, and, determined to clear the hesitation out of her brain, she jumped abruptly out of her chair and pulled herself up straight.

"So! We've got work," she said energetically. "Yes, I mean work. Going home, after all, is a delivery job. We've got to carry ourselves back to Mother. So let's get ready!"

"There you go!" Jiji seconded her energy with restored humor and did a backward somersault. Kiki, too, at last began to feel excited and set busily about her preparation.

"Oh . . . oh, yes, that reminds me, I have to tell Osono."

"Oh, goodness! You're leaving the day after tomorrow? Already? Somehow I thought it was still a long ways off . . . When you say you'll be away for a while, about how long will it be?"

Osono knew that Kiki would be going home to visit eventually, so she wasn't much surprised.

"I'm thinking of about fifteen days. It's been a whole year, you know. So I'd like to rest up a bit and enjoy myself."

After she answered, Osono grinned and poked Kiki's cheek.

"Look at you. You're already looking homesick for your mother. Well, there's nothing wrong with that! But, you know, if you want to know what I think, a good length for a visit home is about ten days. So make your 'a while' short and sweet and come back to us as soon as you can."

Kiki was touched by Osono's words, and it made her clown to cover up her embarrassment.

When Kiki called Tombo to tell him she was leaving, he just seemed full of questions.

"Aren't you lucky. Is it a long trip?" He went on and on, asking about how fast she would fly, what altitude she would fly at, whether there'd be a tail wind, what temperature it was up in the sky, how it felt to fly through the clouds, what the clouds tasted like, and so on. Kiki began to wonder if boys had nothing in their heads but questions. That was Tombo for you, always *studying*! After she hung up, Kiki glared at the phone for a while, feeling oddly dissatisfied.

After that, Kiki called some of her more frequent customers to tell them of her absence, as well as her friend, Mimi. Then she made a sign on heavy paper that said, "Notice: On vacation until further notice. With apologies in advance for the inconvenience." And then, in the bottom corner, she wrote in small letters, "Until further notice means about 10 days."

That night, Kiki said to Jiji, "Tomorrow, we'll clean the office and the next morning we'll leave early. Is that all right with you?"

Jiji was obviously delighted and started meowing with excitement. Trying to catch his tail in his mouth, he ended up running in circles. When he finally stopped, he said, as if he'd suddenly remembered, "What are you going to do about presents for Kokiri and Okino? It wouldn't be a good idea to go back empty-handed, you know."

"Oh, but we've got lots and lots of presents—our stories, you know . . ."

"Is that all you're going to take? What happened to the tummy warmers you were going to knit? You were working on them, weren't you? There was one of blue wool . . ."

Kiki didn't say anything, looking as if Jiji had caught her on the spot.

"What! You didn't finish them? Wouldn't you know! It's just like it was with the herbal medicine. Are you ever going to get any good at things that take time and patience?" Jiji humphed loudly, breathing on Kiki's leg.

"How can you be so mean!" said Kiki, pretending to be hurt, and then, bursting out in a smile, she took a fat paper bag out of the closet.

"Here, let me show you. I did indeed take 'time and patience.'" When she drew her hand out of the bag and opened it, a small tummy warmer fell out onto the floor. It was bright blue with a pattern in silver thread.

"That's yours, Jiji. I made it so you could go home in style. After all, you lost the one Granny made for you, on New Year's Eve."

When Kiki put his new tummy warmer on, Jiji was speechless with happiness. He began to run in circles again.

"And look, I even made them for Mother and Father, too." There were two good-sized tummy warmers, one a bright orange and the other a dark green.

"It was tough, doing all the knitting in secret, you know."

"Hey, that's cheating. Keeping secrets from me."

"But don't you think a good surprise is three times better than knowing ahead of time?"

"A good surprise? Well, I guess so. Hey! That's a good idea."

"What do you mean, a 'good idea'?" asked Kiki, but Jiji avoided her and went happily back to running in circles.

The next day, as Kiki and Jiji were cleaning, Tombo came running in, panting for breath. Then, with a face so flushed she thought he must be angry, he thrust a paper package out at Kiki. "Here."

Kiki opened the package, thinking to herself that she really didn't understand boys, and found it contained a small shoulder bag. It was pink with a picture of a black cat embroidered on it.

"Oh! It's lovely!" Like Jiji the day before, Kiki was speechless. She was so happy that was all she could say.

"Do you like it?"

Kiki could only nod, smiling.

"Good. I'm glad. You keep it," said Tombo, clumsily, watching her shyly from behind his big dragonfly glasses as she put the bag on her shoulder.

"You're leaving tomorrow, huh? Well, have a good trip," he said gruffly. Then, giving Jiji a pat, he ran off as quickly as he had come.

What's the matter with Tombo? wondered Kiki with amazement as he disappeared from sight.

"That was thoughtful of ol' Tombo, to find something with a black cat pattern on it," commented Jiji, hoping Kiki had noticed Tombo's distress.

"I guess you're right," said Kiki, beginning to understand. If Tombo went out and found this as a present for me, she began to think happily, maybe he does think I'm special, after all.

Kiki undid the red button of the bag's flap and found, to her surprise, a small piece of paper inside. It read, "I'll wave to you from the bridge over the Big River. Tombo."

"What's that?" asked Jiji.

"Oh! Nothing in particular. Just something," said Kiki hastily. Returning the note to the bag, she placed her hand over it protectively.

"Let's go!" Kiki called to Jiji the next morning. As she picked up the broom and their bags and prepared to leave, she turned around to take another look at her shop. The red telephone, the desk on its piles of bricks, the map of the city, the narrow stairway, the piles of flour in the corner, and all the little things she had acquired since she'd come to Koriko. Looking at them brought memories of the past flooding back. Tearing herself away, Kiki took a deep breath and repeated in a husky voice, "Let's go."

As Kiki was pinning her notice on the door, Osono came over with a big bag of bread. The baker was with her, holding the baby.

"We've got a delivery job for you, Kiki" joked Osono in a booming voice. "It's to take this bread to your mother. And don't forget to tell her it's from the best bakery in the city of Koriko."

Noticing that Kiki was looking a little down, Osono laughed heartily as if to blow away the tearful moment.

"Now, Kiki, you absolutely must come back here. You know, we're extremely satisfied with having a witch next door. As somebody told me the other day, you know, we begin to feel there's something wrong after three days if we don't see you flying around the skies of this town."

Kiki fought back the coming tears and rushed into Osono's warm embrace.

"Of course, of course, I'll come back!"

Kiki took off steeply into the morning sky, jiggling the packages and presents tied to the broomstick. The town was slightly hidden in the morning fog rising off the ocean. She flew in a great circle, pivoting the clock tower around the city, and then moved down lower and headed for the bridge over the Big River.

There he was. It was Tombo, as he had promised. Astride his bicycle, he stood in the middle of the bridge waving both hands. Kiki waved back.

"Hey, look! It's Tombo," said Jiji in surprise from behind her.

"That's right!" said Kiki, feeling proud.

"Did you know he was going to be there, Kiki?"

Kiki didn't answer Jiji's question directly, but kept waving.

"Aren't you going to go down and talk to him? It's not enough just to wave, is it?"

"No. It's fine, just like this."

Then, waving broadly one last time, Kiki flew twice back and forth over the bridge and then, curving widely left and right, she set her course firmly to the north, picking up speed as they left the city behind them. Tombo grew smaller and smaller in the distance, until he was hidden in the shadow of the bridge.

"Now, our journey really begins," sighed Kiki, once the city was out of sight. They had only to make a beeline for home. The broom flew smoothly. It was now just as good as the broom Kokiri had given her. Kiki realized that the boisterous, bucking broom she'd put together from a new stick and the whisk from her mother's broom last summer had settled down splendidly. It was flying beautifully.

Kiki also began to see that her presence in the city of Koriko had brought a certain happiness and sense of the unexpected to the people who lived there. Osono had told her to come back as soon as she could. She could feel the same message in the present Tombo had given her. And there were people who felt at a loss if they didn't see her flying through the sky. Slowly and steadily, the wind blew her worries and doubts away, leaving them far behind, as she sped along the path toward home.

Kiki and Jiji's journey went much faster than it had a year before.

The sun rose and fell overhead, and the evening star shone out its faint light. By the time the stars were all out in the dark sky, her much-loved hometown loomed into view in a gap among the trees. Lights shone in all the houses lined up quietly along the streets. The air was heavy with the dew of the forest, so different from the air of the city near the ocean. And even more touching was the sight of the bells, still tied to the tops of the tallest trees, gleaming dimly in the starlight.

Kiki headed straight for home on the eastern edge of the town, and stopped in the air over the rooftop.

"That smell! Kiki, it's bean soup!"

"You're right. I thought she might make it. She knows it's our favorite."

Gustily inhaling the delicious and memorable smell, Kiki and Jiji alighted slowly in the garden. Walking quietly, Kiki very gently knocked on the door.

"Come on in," came her mother's voice. "Sorry, I can't put this down just this minute. I'll be right there."

Kiki and Jiji looked at each other and, with a secret nod, opened the door a crack and said in a deep voice like a man's, "Excuse me, ma'am. You have a delivery!"

Kokiri whirled around from her place at the stove. At the same time, Kiki opened the door wide.

"Oh! Kiki! If it isn't Kiki! I didn't think you'd get here until morning!"

Still holding the ladle dripping with soup, Kokiri held out her arms.

"But I was also thinking, 'I bet she comes back after exactly one year.'"

"And I did!" Dropping her baggage and the broom by the door, Kiki ran over to hug her mother.

"There, there, there." Putting her arms around Kiki's shoulders, Kokiri could only say these words over and over and, every time she said it, Kiki nodded, "Yes, yes, yes."

Okino, who had emerged from the next room, could only smile and watch while the two carried on. But, after a while, he finally spoke up, a twinkle in his eye.

"I hope you won't forget me, while you're at it."

"Oh! Father! I'm back," exclaimed Kiki, rushing over to hug him around the neck.

After the first excitement of the reunion was over, the stories began. Kokiri would talk and then Kiki would talk. Okino and Jiji could only watch with amusement from the sidelines. The wells of talk in the two seemed as if they would never dry up.

Then Kiki brought out the bread Osono had sent and the tummy warmers she had knit for her parents.

"Goodness, who ever would have thought our Kiki would learn to knit . . . " marveled Kokiri, trying on her tummy warmer over her dress, and patting her stomach.

"You know, Mother, Granny, who taught me to knit, seemed to have a mysterious power, and I got the feeling that when she knit, she was knitting that power into whatever she was making."

"There are quite a few older people who have that power," remarked Okino, closely examining the tummy warmer in his hands.

As if he had been waiting for his moment, Jiji stretched up to the tabletop and dropped a small lavender-colored shell out of his ear in front of Kokiri.

"Oh! Jiji! You brought me a present too!"

Kokiri was surprised and delighted.

"Well, Jiji, I see you had a surprise of your own in store!" exclaimed Kiki. Jiji turned to Kiki and said in a whisper, "I got it when we were at the seashore last summer. Like you said, 'good surprises are three times better,' right?"

And it *was* three times better. Kokiri gazed in wonder at the shell, holding it on the palm of her hand, turning it over and over, and examining it closely.

"This is a seashell, isn't it? Is the ocean this color?" she asked.

"Yes, in a way. It's like the color of the ocean just before dawn."

Kokiri looked at Kiki and Jiji and said with feeling, "You two certainly did go far away, didn't you? Just to think, it seems only yesterday that you were both babies! And you've now done such a splendid job and you're so grown up!"

Hearing those words, Kiki began to feel a sense of confidence and pride slowly spread out inside her. She had wanted to ask someone whether she had achieved what she set out to do, and now she realized that she had wanted, above all, to ask Kokiri. Kiki saw that it was those words from Kokiri that she had needed most.

Then Kiki said, "You know, Mother. I've been thinking. I've been thinking that sometimes a witch shouldn't always ride around on a broom. Oh, when we have to make deliveries and such, we might have to fly, but sometimes it's better to walk. When you walk, you meet all kinds of people and sometimes you end up talking to them, even if you don't want to. I wouldn't have met Osono if I hadn't been walking. If I'd been flying around to get over my sadness, I might never have found a home.

"From other people's point of view, too, when they see a witch up close, they see for themselves that we don't have hooked noses or hideous grins. And we can talk and get to understand each other better."

"You're right, you know. That's exactly right." Kokiri was

admiring her daughter's growth, and Okino was gazing with surprise as if he was seeing his own daughter for the first time.

From the next morning, Kiki spent the days just like she had as a child.

"How easy it is to go back to being a little girl!" said Kokiri, smiling. "Well, I guess there's no reason why not. You've only been away for a year."

Kiki drank tea from her favorite teacup and tried on her old, fancy dresses in front of the mirror to her heart's content. At night, she went to sleep in the embrace of the same old bedding she'd slept in since the time she was a baby, and stayed in bed as long as she wanted in the morning.

When she had time, she strolled around the town, and people crowded around, asking her questions.

"Oh, Kiki. When did you get back?"

"Hello, Kiki. You're looking very pretty and grown up."

"Hi, Kiki. It's been a long time. Come over and chat sometime."

Everyone was so solicitous and nice, it made Kiki completely happy. It's the kind of warmth you can only find in the town where you grew up.

And yet, after five days had gone by like this, Kiki found her thoughts returning constantly to Koriko: Osono's sonorous laugh; the smell and taste of fresh-baked bread; the people who would strike up conversations with her through her apartment window; the tree-lined path along the Big River; the smell of the ocean; the tall, spindly clock tower; the smiling face of her friend Mimi; and Tombo. The image of Tombo waving as hard as he could from the bridge stayed firmly in her mind, and it seemed to be pulling her back to Koriko. Kiki began to realize there were many things she wanted to tell Tombo when she saw him again.

And what about her business? Maybe there were lots of people calling, needing her services. The more she thought about it, the more she began to feel that, despite the fact that she was back in her hometown, she was only there for a visit. And she began to fidget. She had come to like the city of Koriko very much, even though she had only lived there for a year.

Finally, Kiki said to her parents, "I think I'll go back to Koriko pretty soon, maybe tomorrow or the next day."

"What! We thought you'd stay at least ten days," said Okino with surprise. "Are you getting bored here?"

"Oh, no, it's not that. It's just that maybe I have customers waiting. The telephone may be ringing . . . "

"You can't let that bother you. While you're here, you should just let yourself be here, and not think about it."

"But . . ."

Kiki started to explain and then closed her mouth. Okino and Kokiri had waited a whole year for her to come back, after all. She realized that it had been rather thoughtless of her to start talking about leaving so quickly again.

And then Kokiri, who had been standing nearby, said, "Yes, you'll probably be wanting to get back. It wouldn't do if you didn't like the place where you are living. I remember that when I went home after my first year in this town, I found that I just wanted to get back here as soon as I could. It was an odd feeling. Well, Kiki, after another year passes, you'll just have to come home again."

The next day, Kiki and Jiji flew over to the grassy knoll to the east. Sitting on the slope overlooking the town, they gazed at the beautiful panorama stretching out before them.

"Jiji, I've made up my mind to go back to Koriko tomorrow. That's all right with you, right?"

Jiji was teasing insects in the grass with a front paw. "Sure. Though it seems like we just got here."

"If you're worried about presents, I've already decided what to take."

"Is it a secret this time, too?"

"No. I'm going to take some of Mother's medicine to Osono. The sneeze medicine will come in really handy for the baby. I'm not so sure what to do about Tombo . . . but, I was thinking . . . you know the bells that Mother tied in the treetops? How about taking him one of those? I could take down the biggest one and polish it up until it shines. It's kind of a memento of my girlhood . . . "

"Hmm. I think that's a very good idea. And a lot more thoughtful than a fountain pen," remarked Jiji, nodding.

"Oh! You tease," laughed Kiki.

"The bell makes a pretty sound, so I won't write a poem. I probably couldn't write one anyhow."

The fragrance of the grass rose from beneath their feet. On the breezes that blew over them now and then came the lowing of cows grazing in the pastures around them. Kiki lay down on the grass. When she closed her eyes facing the sunlight, the color of the grass would turn into spots swimming under her eyelids.

It's really wonderful, she thought, to have a place like this to come back to.

When Kiki got back home, Kokiri smiled at her, "Have you been up to the grassy knoll?"

"You can tell?" asked Kiki.

"Oh, yes. You've got the imprint of the grass on your cheek."

That afternoon, Kiki and her mother went and detached the bells from the tops of the trees in the town.

"Whenever the wind would come up this past year, and make these bells ring," said Kokiri, "it reminded us of you." She looked both happy and sad, on the verge of both tears and laughter.

Kiki said, "I suppose it's kind of sad, to think we won't need these bells anymore."

"Oh, no, we'll just put them carefully away until the time comes that we need them again," Kokiri responded.

"Huh?" Kiki couldn't help asking why they would ever need them again. And then Kokiri winked at her and said, "For the time when *your* daughter arrives. She's certain to be as much of a daydreamer as you were."

Kiki kept the biggest bell and, after polishing it carefully, put it in a box to take to Tombo.

So again, Kiki found herself making her farewells to Kokiri and Okino, but this time, she didn't feel as desperate and lonely as she had when she left on her maiden journey a year ago.

"Goodbye now!"

"Goodbye!"

Kiki smiled and waved fondly at her parents, and then she and Jiji set off straight for Koriko. From inside the bag hanging from her broomstick, the bell tinkled now and then. The sound made Kiki speed up even more.

Finally, the sparkle of the ocean appeared in the distance and the buildings of Koriko, like a great pile of square and triangular building blocks, loomed into view.

"There's our . . . town!" said Kiki, pointing.

The shadow of the clock tower stretched over half the city of Koriko in the slanting rays of the evening sun.